Positivity Camp

Sarah Maree

POSITIVITY CAMP

Layout and Publishing by NJ Productions (www.njproductions.us)

Cover illustration by Therro The Kid (@therrothekid)

Map illustration by Nicholas Klein

This book contains the edited version of the original publication on Caffeine is my Muse, an online blog written by Sarah Maree. The type and formatting has been adjusted for ease of reading.

ISBN: 978-1-7348800-0-7

Printed in the United States of America.

First edition: April 2020

A Decree of Dedication

The story started from two to three posts on my blog, but the story quickly grew beyond that. This incredible journey wouldn't have been possible without my sisters' pestering persistence on obtaining the full story. It's thanks to them, and one in particular, that I found the drive to not only finish but to go back and revamp it. This one's for you, sistas!

Also, for my dad who gave me a love of reading, for my uncle who taught me how, and for my husband who gave me confidence.

Table of Contents

PART THREE: EVENING   **94**

PART FOUR: NIGHT   **141**

PART ONE

Morning

CHAPTER ONE

Settling In

My eyes glazed over as I numbly munched on a plain, flavorless bagel. It was too early in the morning for me to deal with any of the nonsense that was happening. I wasn't even awake at this time during the school year, and that had ended a while ago. I tried thinking how much time had passed since school let out for summer, but I was too tired.

Around me was chaos. Some adult, probably the cabin's counselor, droned on and on at the back of the cabin as he explained Positivity Camp's rules, the layout, what parents could expect, and so on. While he talked, the parents fumbled with suitcases, sleeping bags, pillows, and other camping gear as their children cried, screamed, begged, complained, or ignored them. It was clear none of us campers wanted to be here, and it was doubly clear the adults didn't care.

I ignored my cabin's counselor as he rambled. I'd already heard the sales pitch from my school counselor. This camp would change *bad kids*. Actually, they'd specifically avoided saying bad kids. Instead, they'd said the camp would change *misguided* kids and help them become better, kinder, and more aware individuals – whatever that meant. It sounded more like a reform school than an actual camp.

I probably should have paid better attention. If I'd known I'd actually be sent here, I would've stood up for myself more. It figured that the real bully had escaped punishment. Lame.

A paper was thrust into my empty hands. I didn't even remember finishing the bagel.

"Pay attention," my father growled at me.

I wasn't sure if he was upset with me or if he was just as grumpy about being up at this hour as I was. I did my best to look like I cared as I stared at the paper. It was some sort of schedule.

"As we like to say," the counselor said, sounding as though he were wrapping things up, "the skills acquired here last far past the final campfire."

"It's already past 7:45," my mother groaned as she stared at her phone. Several other parents also commented on the time.

"Alright, campers," our cabin's counselor called out. "It's just about time for the parents to head out. Please hand your cell phones and other electronic devices over to them. You'll have stationery to write to them later."

We did a collective groan as parents took our one lifeline away from us. It was too early in the day for us to put up much of a fight. I wondered how the other cabins were handling the sudden technology deprivation.

"Now, it's time to say your farewells. You'll see them and your phones when you graduate in three days. Now, let's turn those frowns upside down." His lack of enthusiasm only made the phrase worse.

We did a collective groan, which went without comment by the adults. Then our parents said their goodbyes and rushed out the door. Before we knew it, we were alone with the counselor. He told us to keep our schedule on us and to prepare for the day's first activities. We had a few minutes where we could finish settling in, but once those minutes were up, he ushered us out the door.

My mind was a foggy mess as we left the cabin. As we stood outside in a mostly single file line, I saw other campers doing the same outside their cabins. From what I could tell, there were other twelve-year-olds in my cabin, but I thought others looked closer to eight. The other cabins looked like they had a range of ages as well. No one looked younger than seven or older than fourteen, though I wasn't sure. I had the vaguest memory of seeing girls, but there weren't any now.

Thinking hurt, so I stopped trying to make sense of things. Our counselor was talking about something, but the only thing I caught from the conversation was *House Joy*. I groaned as I realized that was our cabin's name and he was telling it to us so we wouldn't forget later. I let the thought go. For now, it was easier to accept that I'd been abandoned with a bunch of strangers.

I don't know how long we stood there waiting, but we eventually moved out down a path. Each cabin kept to itself as we marched. I lost track of where we were, mostly because I wasn't trying. When we stopped, I saw that we had assembled under a flagpole. We pledged our allegiance to the American flag as it was raised, then everyone went silent as someone began speaking.

Soon after, we were divided into groups based off our schedules and sent off with a new counselor and group of kids.

CHAPTER TWO

Team Building with Dave

"Alright, Campers! If this is your first time to Positivity Camp, please raise your hand! That's right, raise 'em up!"

Despite being new to the camp, I did *not* raise my hand. Mr. Chipper, as I decided to call him, already had me dreading the camp more than I already had been. I hated the idea that there was a chance to be a return camper.

"Two, four, six, eight...ten!"

There were only twelve of us, I noted with some dismay. I tried finding the other person who hadn't raised their hand, but everyone's hands dropped as the guy continued talking.

"We have ten newcomers. Welcome!"

I gritted my teeth as he clapped enthusiastically for a moment. It was way too early for this kind of upbeat attitude.

"Now, before we get started, are there any questions?" Mr. Chipper looked around excitedly. He started talking before anyone bothered raising their hands again.

"Wonderful! Now, let me go over the camp rules. It's been a busy morning, and I want to make sure you are prepared. As you may have seen upon entering camp, there is only one rule here. Just stay positive by saying only positive words. Super easy, right?"

"Wait, we can't say any of the words on the board outside?" someone asked.

"Ah! And you've just said one."

I tried figuring out which word had been negative. It took me a moment, but I decided it had to be *can't*. At that moment, I decided that keeping my mouth shut would be better than risk saying a negative word.

"We will let it go for now," Counselor Chipper continued without giving any explanation. "But your second use of a forbidden word means watching the positivity video. Really, we can talk about consequences later! For now, just keep saying positive things and staying positive!"

His face looked inhuman with the wide grin he somehow managed to maintain.

"Now that we're done with that, let's work on our team building. Who's ready to start having fun and learning how to be more positive?"

Just three days of this, I repeated the litany over and over to myself.

The counselor went to a bin that rested against the big tree we were all clustered in front of. He rummaged inside it for a bit before he came back over to us. He was still smiling that creepily happy smile.

"Let's start with the name game! That way we can get to know each other's names before we do any of the other activities. I'll go first." He held out a little bean bag ball that he'd taken from the bin. "See this? If the ball is tossed to you, say your name and a way to remember it. Like this." He proceeded to toss the ball up in the air and catch it.

"Hi, Campers!" he called out annoyingly. "My name is Dave. I am a Camp Counselor here at Positivity Camp. The D in my name stands for daring. The A is for adventure. V is for victorious, and E is for exiting! With my adventurous spirit, I feel like exploring the deep blue sea and looking for Davy Jones and his locker. Get it? Dave, Davy? Ah, you'll get the hang of it here in a minute! Alright, now who to pick next?"

Of course, he picked me first. I somehow managed to catch the dumb ball. I chuckled as I realized it wasn't a ball with beans in it but was actually a stress ball. How fitting.

"Do I have to do this?" I stalled as a devious plan formed in my mind.

"Yes, Camper, you have to do this. Now tell us your name. We'll help you from there!"

I sighed, thought about it for a moment longer, and decided a video would be better than the name game. I stood up, the stress ball still in hand.

"Hi, my name is Daniel. D is for disturbed. A is for annoyed." I smiled as I spoke the next line but only because that creepily perpetual smile had disappeared from Dave's face. "N is for naughty." I saw his face turn pale, but I kept right on going. "I is for indifferent.

E is for embattled." I heard someone let out an appreciative "ooh" for that one. "And L is for loathe," I stopped as I forgot who to make my name relate to.

Face burning red, Counselor Dave finally snapped. "To the nurse's office, young man! And be silent on your way there!"

His shrill voice grated on my nerves as he shouted the commands. I casually tossed the ball down to the girl next to me. She caught it and stood as I passed, startling me into stopping.

"Can I go with him?"

"It's *may* I," the man corrected waspishly.

"Oh? Well then, Mr. Dave. If that's going to be your attitude. *Fine.* D is for defective, A is for abhorrent, V is for vile, and E is for egregious! And my name is Wendy. W for wicked, E for execrable, N for negativity, D for deplorable, and Y for ya-hoo!"

I'm pretty sure everyone's jaw dropped as Wendy spoke. I had been lucky enough to watch Dave as she did so. His lips never stopped moving as Wendy rattled off the terrible words. No words formed long enough for him to sputter them out. I could tell some of the words she had used had to have been up on the boards posted outside the camp walls, but the way Wendy wielded them was like watching a master at work! Still, the last one gave everyone pause, including Dave who had been on the verge of recovery. Then again, maybe not.

"What?" Wendy asked, surprised by the confused looks. "Ya-hoo is more than a search engine. Honestly, people! They're a race of brutish, degraded creatures in some guy's book. Look the word up."

"ENOUGH!"

Yup, she broke Dave.

"Both of you! To the Psychiatrist!"

"The what?" Wendy and I said at the same time. I smiled, but quickly bit my lip to hide my amusement.

"THE NURSE!" he shouted at us. "Now," he ordered more calmly but still with a hint of anger. He then pointed at a worn dirt path off to the left of our group.

I didn't wait for him to call us back; I ran for the path to the nurse's office, or was she a psychiatrist? Luckily, I had seen the Nurse's Station earlier, though, that was likely because it happened to be pressed against the entrance where all the forbidden words were posted. I didn't have to look back to know that Wendy had followed after me. When we were out of earshot, I couldn't help but congratulate her on her awesome use of negative words.

"Oh, you shouldn't give me all that much credit. Ha! *Shouldn't.* Anyway, I had my phone and was looking for something for my name. That's how I knew about the ya-hoo people."

"You still have your ph-" I began to ask as I recalled our counselor forcing us to give ours up.

She shushed me and we both looked around nervously. Then she nodded and shot me a wink. A few minutes passed before we felt confident enough to talk again.

"That's still awesome," I said, keeping my voice low.

"Do you know where we're going?" Wendy asked as she looked around at the unfamiliar territory.

"Sort of. I think I see the flag from this morning to the left there. From there I think you can see the Nurse's Station. I know it's near the entrance and the signs."

"Do you think they'll add any of those things to the boards out there?" She grinned impishly as we walked.

"I hope so!"

"You know," she said slowly, "I bet this camp could be pretty fun."

"You can't be serious." I shot her a concerned look for suggesting such an absurdity.

"I am! I mean, can you imagine if we did that every time they talked to us?"

"What? Said a forbidden word? I have a feeling we're going to regret it with that psychiatrist. And the video," I added, suddenly regretting not thinking ahead to that no doubt painful experience.

"No, not that." She bumped my shoulder playfully. "We *follow* the rules from here on out," she suggested with a wink.

"Not sure I'm following." I looked at her suspiciously.

"Trust me," she said with a wink.

There was no time for further conversation as we had reached another group playing the name game. We were silent after that as we didn't want to draw unwanted attention. By the time we passed several other groups, we had reached the Nurse's Station.

CHAPTER THREE

Forbidden Words with Emily

"I've received word about the two of you," someone called out, their voice coming from behind us rather than from inside the building.

I must have jumped because Wendy laughed. I spun around to glare at the nurse, counselor, psychiatrist, or whoever it was who had called out to us.

"I am Counselor Emily."

"I'm Wendy. And yes, we're here to see the video," Wendy said, getting right to the point.

"Before we do that, I need the two of you to come with me." The woman with her khaki shorts and brown collared shirt said as she turned toward the camp's main entrance and walked out.

"Should we follow?" I whispered to Wendy, but she had already started after Counselor Emily. Then I remembered her plan. Or rather, I remembered she had one and that I knew little to nothing about it. With a counselor nearby, there was no way to ask questions safely. Instead, I tried figuring out what Wendy's last cryptic message had meant: *We follow the rules from here on out.*

"Well, nothing better to do," I grumbled under my breath.

As I caught up to Wendy and Counselor Emily, the woman motioned for us to turn around. Then she pointed at the boards hanging up on the sign post outside of camp.

"I want you both to take a good long look at these words. They are to remain out here, and when you enter camp, you are to erase them from your mind. I will give you two minutes to study them."

Two minutes felt like ages to me as I gazed at the pitiful list of words. Really, their one sign felt inadequate for all the *bad* words out in the world. I studied it anyway, intent on being helpful to Wendy with her scheme.

No, not and any contraction thereof, the prefix un-, less than, bad, nasty, awful, terrible, worse, hate, worthless, never, cusswords of any kind, derogatory words such as dumb, stupid, idiot, etc.

As I looked at the main board with its forbidden words, Wendy's message clicked in my head. We could still say plenty of *horrendous* things if we were careful to avoid using the words on the board. My mind drifted as I wondered what would happen to the list if we started *misbehaving.*

Wendy chuckled as though reading my thoughts.

"Is something funny?" Counselor Emily demanded.

I tried to keep from grinning, just so I wouldn't be called on. My mind fumbled for a response other than *no.*

"Yes," Wendy said boldly. I stared at her, confused and concerned. Still, I couldn't fault her for going with the safer answer.

"Oh? Care to share?" Counselor Emily smiled wickedly at her, but Wendy didn't back down.

"At this time, I feel it is best to keep my response quiet."

Counselor Emily stared at Wendy in open-mouthed bewilderment. She tried several times to formulate a comeback, but the perfect answer had her stumped. Wendy shot me a wink and a wicked smile.

I realized then that I'd been thinking about things all wrong. True, we could still say some *rotten* words, but we could be just as chaotic if we said things correctly, too.

"That's all for now, I think," Counselor Emily said, finally regaining her composure. "I do believe it's time for you to see Nurse Pamela for the positivity video." She didn't wait for a response from either of us. She simply turned around and walked back into camp.

Before I could walk under the giant wooden board that separated normal society from the reality of the camp, Wendy bumped into me. "Yahoo," she whispered as she walked past. I smiled, thinking of all the words not on their list. Wendy had been right. Maybe Positivity Camp could be fun.

CHAPTER FOUR

Music with Melinda

My brain felt like mush after being forced to watch what had to be the stupidest video ever. I couldn't even recall what Wendy and I had done to deserve watching the awful thing. Regardless of what we *had* done, I knew what we had to do now. Best of all, if we were clever about it, we wouldn't even be breaking the rules, and that meant no more trips to go watch some stupid camp video.

At the end of the video, the nurse or psychiatrist – I still had no idea which – came in and gave us a brief lecture. As soon as I saw her nametag, I lost all focus. She had come in and introduced herself as Counselor Pamela, but her nametag had Pam on it. Whoever she was, she was all sorts of confusing.

When we left, Wendy filled me in on what I had missed due to Nurse/Psychiatrist/Counselor Pam/Pamela's confusing identity. Apparently, we had to walk to the stage area where we had started the day with our parents and stay there for Counselor Melinda's lesson. Since we had missed the shifting of the groups as campers went to their next activity, we were to catch up with our group there.

All we had to do now was make it through whatever lesson Counselor Melinda had in store for us. In too short of a time, we made it to the camp's stage. Our group sat on the benches, bored expressions on their faces. Although I wasn't looking forward to the new activity, I was happy to see someone other than Counselor Dave in charge. In his place stood Counselor Melinda. Instead of the naming ball, she had clipboards and pens for each of us. Other than that, it looked much the same: bored kids listening to some overly cheerful adult.

"Hey! So glad you two could join us!" Counselor Melinda called out as we approached. "We were just talking about the benefits of being positive, but then you two just learned all about that with our Positivity Camp video, I'm sure," she paused as though waiting for some affirmation.

This time, I beat Wendy to the punch. "You *know* it!"

To my surprise and delight, Counselor Melinda gave me a suspicious look as though she were trying to discern if I were being sincerely cheerful or if I had just used the forbidden word *no*. Not that it would have made any grammatical sense if I had.

"You *know* we did!" Wendy called out a mere second behind. We exchanged mischievous smiles. Clearly the video had done little to curb our negative tendencies.

"Alright." Counselor Melinda lost her smile as she eyed us suspiciously. "I see you two should be separated. Ike, you pair up with Wendy, and Meliah, you team up with Daniel."

How did she know our names? The question went unanswered as I realized Wendy and I wouldn't be partners anymore. I wandered over to sit with Meliah and watched in dismay as Wendy went in the opposite direction to sit with Ike. She shot me an encouraging wink, but it hardly registered. I wanted to be *her* partner, not Meliah's.

"Now then, we were just about to take what we learned and put it into song!" Counselor Melinda smiled vibrantly at everyone, clearly intending to do the positive thing and move on. "Now that you are teamed up with your buddy, it's time to work together and come up with a positive song about what you've learned here at Positivity Camp. So, put your knowledge to the test, and see what you can remember thus far. Oh, and if you would rather do a poem, that works too!"

Despite the setback, my brain was working overtime. "Hey, Meliah?" I began cautiously. Wide-eyed, she stared at me before shyly replying with a barely audible yes. "Do you mind if we write our ideas down separately and then compare?"

"No," she said shyly. Her eyes widened in terror a moment later as she realized her error. Despite the awkward delay, she quickly worked to slur the word into something else. "*Ow!* Now…" she repeated, somewhat successfully turning her *no* into a *now*. "Now, that sounds fun," she said with a nervous laugh.

For everyone's sake, Wendy and I had to bring down the camp and its stupid rules. No one should have been fearful of saying *no* to someone else. We had to show them that their own rules were counter to their stupid philosophy or whatever it was they followed.

That in mind, I sat down and began writing; however, all I could come up with was a semi-catchy phrase that hardly made any sense.

Regardless, it would at least irritate them. Still, I needed more.

"Hey, Meliah? Do you mind if we merge ours? I have a fun catchy...um...chorus," I stammered as I tried coming up with something that sounded like I had actually tried doing the assignment. "But that's it."

"Sure!"

The poor girl looked enthused. Too bad she had no idea what I was planning. Part of me felt bad, but only a little, since I knew where the blame would fall.

"Time's up, everyone! Let's have Daniel and Meliah go first."

I couldn't believe my luck! We were going first! I tried not to smile as we made our way up to the front row of long benches. Meliah had her clipboard and I had mine. We each had the same words, but not the same intentions. Again, I felt bad for the deception, but quickly focused on the task at hand.

"Uh," Meliah began shyly. "This is our knowledge song. It's a little interactive..." Melian's voice died away and she began blushing furiously.

"So please do your part and chant or sing along!" I finished for her. I couldn't believe my luck, I hadn't intended for anyone to sing along with us. Meliah was turning out to be a better partner than I'd thought, and for once, I felt perfectly comfortable in front of a group. Of course, Wendy's approving and downright mischievous smile helped too.

"When you hear a rule you know," I explained, "just say 'know, know knowledge!' to show your knowledge of all that you know!"

"Uh, I'm nnnn." Counselor Melinda began to protest, but when she began saying a forbidden word, her response turned to a humming sound as she tried finding an alternative N word for *not*.

"We must obey the many rules," Meliah began softly, completely unaware of Counselor Melinda's continuous humming.

When no one spoke, I quickly rushed in, "Remember to say *know* to all you know!"

"Know, know knowledge," Wendy chimed in at last.

"We must be positive in thought, and word, and deed," Meliah continued, this time sounding a bit more confident.

"Know, know knowledge," Wendy and several others chimed in along with me.

"We must speak only positive words and avoid the forbidden ones."

"Know, know knowledge!" This time everyone chimed in, except for Counselor Melinda, who was still humming.

"We are here to have positive fun."

"Know, know knowledge!"

"We are here to learn."

"Know, know knowledge!"

"We are here to be more positive."

"Know, know knowledge!"

By the time the final chorus ended, Counselor Melinda found her voice. "Is that all you have?" she demanded. "You two certainly are *knowledgeable*! And now you can go show your knowledge to the nurse! I had hoped you would have learned your lesson the first time, Daniel," she said more calmly, "but you, Meliah?" She shook her head in disappointment.

"Excuse me, Counselor Melinda," I interjected, "but why are you sending us to the nurse?" I played innocent, but poor Meliah was in tears. Honestly, she had nothing to worry about.

"Why? WHY?! Because you broke a rule!"

"What? When we said we know things? But that was what you told us to do! To share the knowledge we had learned."

"I-I!" she stammered for several seconds as she sought a proper rebuttal.

"Perhaps *you* should go see the nurse," someone suggested from the benches.

Counselor Melinda whirled around to confront the culprit, but the camper wisely remained quiet and avoided eye contact.

"All of you are just as guilty!" she fumed.

"Counselor Melinda, what is going on here?" The new, deeper voice startled everyone into looking up at the top of the hill where Head Counselor Petrel could be seen walking down the earthy steps.

"Ah! Mr. Petrel," Counselor Melinda said with a strange look. "You two," she said, turning on us, "hand me your papers."

I happily handed mine over, and when Meliah remained frozen, I gently took her clipboard from her and handed it over as well.

"Read it, and you'll see why I am sending them to the psychiatrist's office," Counselor Melinda handed the papers over. She gave me a smug look before Mr. Petrel could see, but I kept my expression blank.

"I see," Mr. Petrel said after reading through both copies. "Music lessons are over, children," he said sternly.

Counselor Melinda smiled.

"You will proceed to the kickball field where you will find Mrs. Tammy." As he spoke, the smile disappeared from Counselor Melinda's face.

"What? But they should go to the nurse's office, or at least stay here. What about my hour?"

"Your hour. Is over," Mr. Petrel answered stiffly. "Off you go, children."

There was a menacing way he said those last few words that had us all scrambling to get out of there as fast as possible. Not even Wendy had braved lingering around the head counselor.

CHAPTER FIVE

Word Spreads

Everyone stayed silent as we escaped from Head Counselor Petrel. The silence only lasted as long as it took to get out of sight, and that ended the second we reached the top of the stairs. Several other campers tried talking to me, but I kept running. I wanted to catch up to Wendy and find out what song she had prepared.

"Wendy!" I called out as loud as I dared. Luckily, she heard me and slowed down enough for me to catch up. Then we were walking at a more normal pace.

"What is it?"

"I…wanted," I said, trying to catch my breath. "I wanted to know what you came up with. I nnnnoticed," I stammered in an attempt to cover up the forbidden word *never*. "That I was the only one to present."

"You and *Meliah*, you mean," Wendy said stiffly.

Was she jealous? I tried not to smirk at the thought.

"Yeah, but I want to know what *you* did."

Wendy looked around, and I suddenly noticed we were surrounded by nearly all the campers from our group. Several looked away in an attempt to be inconspicuous, but the rest continued their blatant eavesdropping. I saw no reason to be concerned. Some of them were even smiling.

"Fine," Wendy said at last. "But you should curb your excitement. Ike and I struggled to come up with anything. I was too focused on using knots somehow, but how do you talk about camp knowledge using a boating term?"

"A boating term?" one of the eavesdroppers asked. They were met with a glare from Wendy. I tried looking menacing too, but all I could think of was that Wendy had accidentally added an *s* to *not*, but that didn't make sense. Unless she meant tying a knot?

"Yes, the speed of a boat can be measured in either miles per hour or in knots. Of course, I also thought about knots in terms of tying rope, but that hardly would have worked to describe this place and all the things we *know*," she ended with a smile and a sly wink at me.

"That still sounds great," I said encouragingly. "Maybe we can use that later…for something."

"That's true."

"You guys are going to keep saying things?" one kid asked excitedly.

"You'll get us all in trouble," another complained.

"HEY!"

The shout made our entire group pause. We'd just left the flag-pole lot and were following a dirt path to the main asphalt road. Farther down the main path, a different group of campers were shouting and waving at us.

"Should we make a run for the kickball field?" someone, possibly Ike, asked Wendy.

"We wait by the dirt path," she replied.

"Hey!" The boy stopped and panted as he tried catching his breath. He had left the rest of his group far behind. The kid knew how to sprint! If we had any capture the flag games later, I wanted him on my team.

"What is it?" Wendy asked, once again taking charge.

"We…we were in art class….drawing things…burning wood… Teach…Teacher," he clarified before coughing and clearing his throat. "Teacher stopped. He had to make a special sign…We're going to…put it up now. Had to warn you."

"What?" the question came from several campers behind me. We all leaned in closer.

"New words. *Forbidden* words. They're going up on the wall outside camp. Wanted to warn you." The kid's panting slowed as he finally caught his breath.

"Do you know what they are?" Wendy asked.

"Yeah, but…"

"But they're forbidden now," I finished for him. "Hey, do you remember *all* of them?" I asked, suddenly remembering a way he might be able to confirm my suspicions.

"Yeah, but…"

"If you take the first letter of the words, do they spell Wendy, Daniel, and…what was that counselor's name?" I asked, turning to

Wendy.

"Dave," the kid answered before either of us could remember. His eyes went wide and they flicked about the group before settling on me again.

"You know the story?" I asked, confident I already knew the answer. He nodded slowly a moment later, confirming my suspicions. With a wicked smile, I pointed first at myself and then at Wendy. "Daniel and Wendy," I said, still smiling.

The kid's jaw dropped. Then he was off. He ran past two other campers as he dashed back to spread the word. His group gave us a weary look before passing by us on their way to go place the signs.

Once again, I found myself admiring the kid's speed. If this camp had capture the flag, I *definitely* wanted him on my team.

"That. Was. Awesome!" Wendy shouted gleefully.

I couldn't have agreed more!

"We have art class?" Ike asked, suddenly appearing beside Wendy. I tried shooting him a dirty look for ruining our moment, but then Wendy took off running.

"Come on! I want to see the kickball field!"

She was lying and we all knew it, but the whole group ran after her. We all wanted to see what would happen next.

CHAPTER SIX

Kickball with Coach Tammy

We hadn't been running long when someone called out for us to stop.

"What is it?" Wendy asked as the rest of the group caught up to us.

"Does anyone know *how* to get to the kickball field?"

I looked at Wendy for answers since I had no idea where it was. In fact, I didn't even know the camp *had* a kickball field until a few minutes ago. Judging by the way everyone was looking around, including Wendy, no one else knew either. There were too many trees everywhere for us to see anything that wasn't in the main part of camp.

"I do," a quiet voice interjected before anyone spoke up. A girl raised her hand shyly and we all turned to look at her.

"It's...uh. It's that way." She pointed in the direction we had already been going in. "The...the field has a rock-climbing tower," she said quietly.

"We have a rock wall?" the guy next to her asked, shocked.

"Looks like it," I said, seeing the top of the tower through the trees. It was the first time I had seen it though. If nothing else, it certainly made finding the field easier.

"Yeah, but I mean... *This* place has something *that* cool?" he clarified.

"I doubt we can use it, knowing this place," Wendy added glumly.

"It...um."

We all turned to look back at the shy girl from before. She was digging a hole in the dirt with the tip of her shoe and wasn't making eye contact. "It's from...from the old camp. There are kayaks and obstacle course type stuff, too."

"That explains it," Wendy said.

"Yeah, but considering what we've seen of *this* camp thus far…" I said, letting everyone else fill in the rest, which was probably a good thing too, considering I would have likely said some forbidden word had I kept going with that train of thought.

"Let's get moving," Wendy said, taking charge once more. "We're almost there."

A quick jog had us at a dirt path through the trees. Further in, we had to take a wooden staircase down a steep hill. Then we were in the kickball field, though it was much larger than any kickball field I had ever seen. Looking at the clearing closer, it looked just like a baseball diamond. It had the bases, the diamond shape, everything. So why had they called it a kickball field? Were they that clueless on fun activities?

There were at least twenty kids spread out in the field with even more clustered in a small section near the tower, which was admittedly looking pretty cool. At least, what I could see of the rock-climbing tower looked impressive. I had thought the thing would be old and run down with chunks missing out of it and ivy all over, but from this distance, it looked well maintained. There was hope for this camp after all. Well, if they let us use it anyway.

"We should go around and avoid the group playing kickball," Wendy said. We followed as she took off at a run.

"You're the group of troublemakers," the kickball coach, or counselor, or whatever her title was, called out as we approached. "I'm Coach Tammy," she said as she left her spot with the other group of campers and came to confront us. "You're early," she said matter-of-factly.

"We were sent here," someone from our group called out boldly.

"I'm aware. Had you behaved yourselves, you could have finished your lessons with Counselor Melinda before coming here. Had you done that, you would have been on time. Now, I expect you to wait your turn quietly and respectfully under the tower. Is that understood?"

There were several vague answers which only seemed to aggravate Coach Tammy.

"But we are on time," someone from the back whined.

"What was that?"

No one said a word. I didn't blame the kid for speaking up. He was right, we were on time, but it was clear Coach Tammy had meant we were too early rather than too late.

"I asked you a question."

She was mad now! We all looked around in confusion. None of us were brave enough to correct her, not that it would have been easy to do while trying to avoid using *negative* words.

"Is that understood?!" she asked, her question snapping us to attention…mostly.

"Yes, Coach Tammy!" we shouted, though not in the least bit in unison. Somehow our pitiful effort satisfied her because she turned away and went back to barking orders at the other group of campers.

Not wanting to further aggravate Coach Tammy, we wandered over to quietly sit under the tower. It didn't take long for us to get bored and start talking, especially since there was no way to climb the tower. There were thick wooden doors that covered the hand holds for the beginning portion of the rock wall, and those doors, unfortunately, had several locks on them.

"Can you imagine what else they have here?" someone asked as they stared up at the tower.

"It's so lame they have all those locks," someone else chimed in.

Several of us grumbled our agreement.

"Did you two really get those words removed?" The question immediately sparked interest.

"It sounds like it," I said as I pulled bits of grass from the ground.

"We simply used words that were free game. They became forbidden only because Counselor…" Wendy paused. This time she had been the one to forget Dave's name.

"Dave, like Davy Jones' locker," I grumbled, feeling more than a little irritated that I had remembered his ridiculous trick for remembering names.

"Right," Wendy said slowly. "Anyway, Counselor Dave heard some words that he found to be rather…mmm…. atrocious. Hopefully that word is still free to use," she said with a sigh.

"Not for long," I said, giving her an encouraging wink. She and several others laughed.

"This is so amazing! Do you really think those words are up on the wall outside of camp?"

"I doubt they lied," I said with a shrug.

"There's only one way to find out," one of the girls said, standing.

"What do you mean?" Meliah asked her, a look of concern on her face.

"I mean, there's only one way to find out and that's to go see the board for myself. I'll report back when I have an answer."

"Wait, what?" Meliah stole the words right out of my mouth. "Where are you going? Kayla!" Meliah whispered harshly as Kayla snuck around the tower and disappeared into the woods behind it.

"Well, I doubt we'll be seeing her again," Ike said from his spot against the tower.

"Kayla?" Meliah whispered, tears in her eyes.

The shy girl from before went to stand beside Meliah. "I…uh… I'm sure she'll be alright. She…she looked confident." She smiled at Meliah, but the words only made Meliah look more worried. "I'm, Abigail," the shy girl said, stretching out her hand.

"Alright!" Coach Tammy called out, causing several of us to jump, and poor Abigail to fall down…somehow. None of us had noticed the kickball game had ended and the other group of campers had already started making their way off the field. By the way they were separating, it looked more like there had been two groups.

"Split into two even numbered teams!" Coach Tammy shouted at us. "It's time for kickball!"

"We have an odd number, Coach," Wendy said, coming to the rescue as we all froze in our panic. Without Kayla, our group would be odd numbered, something an informed counselor would likely find suspicious.

"Then one group will have an extra player," Coach Tammy said condescendingly. She was about to say more but did a quick count instead. "Are you trying to be sassy with me?" she suddenly demanded of Wendy.

"Uuuuh," Wendy tried answering, but without being able to say *no*, she struggled to reply properly. "What do you mean?" she asked instead.

"You have an even number. ALL groups have an even number! That way campers always have someone to buddy up with in case of an emergency. Now, were you being smart with me?" Coach demanded again.

"I think she forgot that Meliah and Abigail had gone to the restroom earlier, but they're back now," I lied, jumping to Wendy's defense. "Coach Tammy, Sir!" I added as an afterthought.

Coach narrowed her eyes at me suspiciously, but I held my ground. All the adults seemed to be looking at me that way recently. The thought almost made me smile…almost.

"I expect the person asked the question to do the answering," she said coldly. "What's your name?"

"Daniel," I said, trying my best not to lose my temper at Coach Tammy's continually scornful tone and abrasive attitude.

"Thought as much." She turned away from me then and focused on someone else. "You two," she said, pointing at Ike and the shy girl, Abigail, "pick your teams and get out on that field!"

"Yes, Coach Tammy!" our group shouted in complete discord.

"Wait, Coach Tammy," Ike said, looking at the rest of us, which was probably for the best since he didn't see Coach Tammy's face redden. "There are nooooo-" we all stared helplessly at Ike as he struggled to find a word to replace the forbidden *no*, "-uuuuum-bers…" he said, slurring the two words together. I was just glad he had finally found something that would work. The word had been dragging on for way too long. "Uh," he continued, "our numbers are off."

"Ike," Coach Tammy began.

"I mean that there are…too few to properly play. You need three people for the bases, a pitcher, a catcher, and a few kids for the out-field. We dooooooo have a…uh…shortage of players."

"I am aware of that."

"Oh."

"You are to play with the number you have. The other group that was to be joining us has other obligations at the moment. *Now pick your teams.*"

"Yes, Coach Tammy!" Ike and Meliah shouted.

As much as I disliked Ike, I couldn't blame him for trying.

There was no time after that for any of us to talk, other than for picking teams. Even so, I still wanted to know who else had left? And when? But all I received for my covert questioning looks were equally covert looks of confusion or discreet headshakes. No one knew, and even if they did, they couldn't say without getting us all in trouble. Regardless, we were in this together now.

CHAPTER SEVEN

Abigail's Message

Playing kickball turned out to be more fun than I thought it would be. While the game was fun, the situation was not. The game kept us all separated and unable to talk, even when the teams switched positions and my group left the field for our turn to kick. It just wasn't possible, not with Coach Tammy looming nearby. When she wasn't barking orders at other people, she was staring at either Wendy or me.

Just when I had given up all hope of doing anything other than kickball, Coach Tammy's radio went off. Her name was repeated several times before she grumbled and stormed off the field.

"What's that about?" the kid next to me asked.

"Wish I knew," I responded back.

"Do you think-?"

I shushed him harshly. I couldn't hear what was being said with him talking in my ear.

"What? Repeat again. Over," Coach Tammy shouted into her radio.

"What's going on?" someone else asked.

I looked around me. No one was playing kickball anymore, and the other team was running in to find out what was going on. I guess we were all curious to know, and we were too curious to care about the consequences. At least, my team was supposed to be where we were, but Wendy was on the other team. I frowned but kept listening despite my concerns.

"Repeat again. Over." There was a pause then garbled static that I doubted anyone around me could understand. "Are you sure? Over." Coach had her back to us as she continued shouting her questions.

Without warning, Coach Tammy slammed the radio back into its holster at her hip and whirled around. There were several gasps as we were all caught off guard by the action.

"Listening in, were we?" Her tone was cold as she gave us all a level look. "That saves me some time then. You are all to go immediately to the Art Barn." Coach paused as she looked at her watch and frowned "Our time was up four minutes ago, so you're all late. I suggest you hurry. Oh, off with you. Now!"

There were a few chuckles as several of us realized that Coach Tammy, a real stickler for being on time, had made *us* late thanks to what appeared to be a broken relic...a watch.

"Hey!" Coach Tammy's voice called out as a few in the group started taking off for the only path in or out of the field. "The barn is that way." She pointed at a hill on the other side of the field. "Up the *hill* is a game path. Take that to the left and you'll be at the Art Barn. You have two minutes. Go!"

"Two minutes?" the kid in front of me groaned as I sprinted past him.

"Who uses watches anymore?" someone else snickered as they started running. The comment had a few laughing, but most of us concentrated on running.

"MOVE!" The command sounded like a thunderclap, but it had the desired effect as it forced the rest of the group into a run.

As soon as I cleared the field and made it to the very ill used animal path, I stopped running. Several others stopped with me. The trees and bushes gave us enough cover from Coach Tammy, but when I looked back to see where she was, the field was empty of all but a few stragglers from our group.

"Where...where'd she go?" I asked in a rush as I caught my breath.

"I...I...oh, who cares?" Wendy sounded as out of breath as I felt.

"We...we'll be late," Meliah said from her spot next to Wendy.

"Technically," I said, my breathing finally under control, "we're already late."

"He's right. We may as well catch our breath," Wendy added.

"What...what do...do you think...happened...to...to Kayla?" Abigail asked in her halting speech. I honestly couldn't tell if she was still being shy or if the run had stolen her breath too. Regardless, she still wouldn't look at anyone when she spoke.

"I'm sure - I'm sure she's fine," Meliah smiled as she spoke. "She and whoever went with her."

"Yeah, but we may have trouble if we are later than expected," I warned them.

"Right, let's move." Wendy started us all off at a brisk pace down the path. It was slow going as we had to go single file.

We were only a few minutes late to the barn. Before we entered, Abigail spoke again. Apparently, she had been trying to say something, but had been too shy.

"But...Meliah...but."

"What is it? We really ought to go in." Meliah looked around.

Several of us, Wendy included, had stopped to hear what the shy girl had to say. Some of us obviously didn't care about getting in trouble.

"I...it's...I...it's just that...what if we *gained* a new member," Abigail said, biting her lip in concern.

I looked around to make sure I wasn't the only one stunned and was happy to see several others looking as confused as I felt. A few looked around, concerned.

"Abigail, who's the new kid? Who joined us?" Wendy asked quickly.

"You're late, *children*."

We turned to see the art counselor watching us from the doorway of the barn.

"You can call me, Teacher. Off to your seats, please. There are a few empty stools left. Tardiness is very rude, as is talking when there are things to be done," with that said, he waved at us to enter the barn.

"Sorry-"

"Enough," Teacher said with a frown. "Talking is prohibited until your work is done. Is that understood, children?"

"Yes, Sir," I said quickly. At the same moment, I felt Wendy's elbow in my ribs. She had tried to warn me, but sadly it had come too late. A few others spoke up too. We were all awarded with a shake of Teacher's head.

"A pity." As he spoke, Teacher clasped his arms behind his back. "That. Is strike one. You would be wise to avoid another. Now, to your seats. There is work to be done."

I clamped my mouth shut. Whatever fantasy I had of enjoying a peaceful time at the Art Barn vanished in that moment. The only thing I could concentrate on was not earning a second strike. I had thought I had seen the worst of the camp's punishments, but having Teacher against me certainly felt worse than having to endure ten of the stupid introductory / punishment videos.

CHAPTER EIGHT

Art with Teacher

Making art in silence was *not* my idea of fun. Even the birds were noticeably quiet as we all worked. Surprisingly, Teacher's assignment had been an actual art assignment: Draw a living creature. I had been expecting some sort of punishment, like etching "I will not be late" into some giant wood block or something. Although, it would probably be more like "I will be on time" since they wouldn't want us writing *not*.

Man, I really hated this place!

And the silence! Some kid had already been given a warning for swiveling his stool and making it squeak. Now, we all sat stiffly for fear of squeaking. It was so frustrating! The camp had been bad enough when it came to taking simple every day, yet *somehow*, negative words away from us. Now they were taking *all* of them away.

Worse yet, we had some unknown imposter in our group. After what shy girl Abigail had said, it made sense that someone had joined us rather than leaving. And where was that one girl? Kayla, was it? Where did she go? When would she be back?

"What's this?" Teacher demanded from directly behind me.

I jumped in my stool, which was not something I thought would be physically possible. My pencil stopped moving as I slowly swiveled around to answer the question. The action caused the ridiculous stool to squeak, but I ignored it.

"That, is strike number two."

My jaw dropped in surprise. "What is? The drawing? Wait, the chair squeaking?" I cursed the wobbly seat beneath me, but Teacher was looking at my sketch and not my chair.

"Yes." The word came out calmly, with no hint of emotion behind it whatsoever.

I had to clamp my mouth shut as Teacher turned his attention away from my sketch to stare at me. I so desperately wanted to tell him that was *two* things and thus strike two *and* three. Luckily, I managed to keep quiet, though I did wonder how long it would be until I managed a third strike. Teacher's look clearly showed his disdain.

"Dispose of that garbage," Teacher ordered with a flippant wave of his hand. Then he turned, his hands clasped behind his back once more.

"What's wrong with it?" I had done it now! But seriously, there was nothing wrong with what I was drawing. True, the woman had no clothes, but that was how all my drawings started out. First I drew the basic form, then the clothes, then details and so on. It wasn't like there *were* any details yet. Just the basic outline. I hadn't even done anything perverted with it, either.

"*That* is inappropriate content for a young man to be drawing. *Dispose of it*," Teacher ordered once more.

"But there's nothing bad about it!"

There were several gasps as Teacher stopped walking and turned around to face me directly. Even on the stool, he loomed over me. With his black painter's apron on, he looked like some evil beast. For several long seconds he glowered down at me. Then he spoke in that same quiet and controlled voice, "Strike three."

"For arguing?" That little voice in my head kept telling me to shut up, but I couldn't let it go. I had to know what was so bad about my art.

"For the forbidden word."

I went over the conversation in my head before I realized what I had said. *Bad*, I had said *bad*. I shook my head as my brain sorted it all out. After only a few seconds I had several replacement words lined up. If only I had said one of those instead!

"Since this is your first offense with me, you are to report to the Nurse's Station." Teacher leaned in closer and I leaned away, my back resting painfully against the edge of the table. "Come here again and utter a forbidden word, and you'll learn what true art is."

That dead tone of his terrified me as much as his words. I was about to slither off my stool and leave when someone spoke up.

"But that isn't fair!"

It was Wendy! Wendy had spoken, but what was she thinking? Not only had she argued back, but she had used a forbidden word too.

"Young lady. If you think I am fooled by your attempt to join your college in his punishment, then you are sorely mistaken." Teacher settled back into his customary stance as he spoke to Wendy. "I have been warned about the two of you. From this moment on, you are to be separated. Tammy should have done so earlier, but it seems the message went astray. Regardless, rules must be followed. You," Teacher said as his arm shot out and his finger pointed at one of the campers from my group. "Accompany Daniel to the Nurse's Station." Teacher's hand dropped back to his side as he turned to face Wendy. "As for you. You are to sit outside at the back of the barn, alone, on the tree stump, until I can decide what to do with you."

There was a moment of silence as everyone froze, but then the kid who had been chosen to be my escort swiveled around. The stool, of course, elicited a screech of protest, and to my delight, Teacher cringed at the sound. As an added insult, I shifted my weight and made mine screech as well. I didn't need to look back to know Wendy was also on the move as her stool let out a shrill cry.

The act of defiance was pitiful, to say the least, but it was the only thing any of us dared do. I didn't even get to say goodbye to Wendy as she had to take a different door out of the barn, nor did I dare look in her direction for fear Teacher would worsen her punishment. I hated to think that she would be punished because of me, but I didn't know what to do. She *had* deliberately gotten herself in trouble. Maybe that meant we were still in this together?

As I walked to my doom, I tried stifling the guilt I felt, lest it dissuade me from my goal. No. From *our* goal. The camp rules *had* to be broken.

CHAPTER NINE

Positivity Video with Nurse Pam

"So sad to see you back here again and so *soon*."

The smug look on Counselor Emily's face had to go. I debated glaring at her but decided to keep quiet instead.

"Did you run into trouble with Teacher?"

That did it!

"Trouble's a strong word, but I suppose I can see what you mean. He *is* troublesome. I'll let him know you said that next time I see him." Now, I was the one smirking. My grin only widened as the kid next to me let out a whistle of approval.

"You-I-that's…but…and," Emily sputtered as we passed her and went up the steps to the Nurse's Station. She was still talking when the door closed behind us, ending whatever rebuttal she might have had. It was a small victory, but I enjoyed it, nonetheless.

I didn't get to enjoy it for too long, however, because Nurse (or Psychiatrist) Pamela (or Pam) was inside waiting for us, or rather, she was waiting for me.

"Back again so soon?" She looked genuinely perplexed.

"Yeah, Teacher insulted my art, and I slipped up. Guess being… *bitter*," I cringed at my poor word choice, but there was little help for it, "makes for a bitter response." I would have used *negative* instead but couldn't remember if it was on the board or not. *No,* I thought after a quick mental recap, *negative wasn't on the board, but negativity was.* I was fairly confident of that, considering it was one of the words Wendy had used against Counselor Dave. It was too late to change my word choice now, so I decided to save the word for some later use.

"You're walking a fine line, young man," she warned.

I stared at her for a moment, then at her nametag. It was bothering me that she had introduced herself as Pamela, but her nametag still read Pam. I *had* to know the truth! Besides, what was there to lose in asking?

"Are you a nurse or a psychiatrist? Is your name Pam or Pamela?"

"What?"

"I keep hearing you called both a nurse and a psychiatrist, and you said your name was Pamela, but your name-tag says Pam. So, which is it?"

She sighed before giving me a long unreadable look. "Just call me Nurse Pamela."

Gah! She was so frustrating! Just like this camp. Suddenly, something clicked in my head, and before I could stop myself, I spoke. "You're the epitome of what is wrong with this place."

"Excuse me?" she asked, her bent nose crinkling with her confusion.

"Confusing," I said. "You're probably both a nurse and a psychiatrist–"

"Young man."

"–and your name is both Pam and Pamela."

"Young man!"

"You're just like the words! The positive ones can be negative, and the negative ones can be positive." I really hoped that I was right about *negative* not being a forbidden word.

"Young man!"

"What?"

"You will take a seat. Now, I had thought you would have grown up and learned your lesson the first time. I am sorely disappointed in you."

"Wow," I said slowly.

Nurse Pamela raised her chin and looked at me down her crooked nose.

"That was so negative."

Nurse Pamela's jaw dropped and her shoulders slumped. "That word," she said slowly, "is forbidden."

"Is it? You may want to check the board again, 'cause you're wrong," I said before turning away and sitting down in the same chair I had sat in earlier that day. The chair next to me remained empty, a clear reminder of what my blunder with Teacher had cost me. Not that it mattered. Teacher had said there were orders to have Wendy and I separated. It had only been a matter of time. Fools. We could cause double the trouble separated.

"I will be checking the board," Nurse Pamela declared. "You! What's your name?"

I turned to look at the poor kid who had escorted me to my punishment. He hadn't said a word on the way over, and now he had Nurse Pamela's full attention. I hoped he could sit outside and watch the grass grow instead of watching the video. Anything was preferable to watching the video. I should have known better.

"It's Brian."

"Well, take a seat Brian."

"But…"

There was a moment of tense silence as Nurse Pamela stared Brian down. Poor kid.

"Yes, ma'am," Brian said as he dragged his feet over to the empty chair. It screeched as he slumped into it. He looked miserable as he stared at his sandals. It was so melodramatic, I almost laughed.

"You will *both* watch the video." Nurse Pamela hit play and left the room.

Brian watched his feet the whole time. I'm pretty sure he had some inner dialogue going on between his toes. I imagined his feet were at war and his toes were soldiers. It was awesome. Neither of us even noticed the video playing in the background.

CHAPTER TEN

The Dining Hall

"I hope you learned what Positivity Camp is really about...*This time around*," Nurse Pamela said sweetly as she reentered the room. I looked up in time to see that the video had stopped playing. Somehow, she hadn't noticed that Brian and I had been staring at his toes for the past forty minutes.

Brian and I exchanged quick glances. All I remembered was his feet and the Toe Wars, as I now called it. A moment of understanding passed between us, and we both kept quiet.

"Excellent," Nurse Pamela said triumphantly. She looked down at her watch.

What was it with adults and their watches? They still had their cell phones, didn't they? I decided to keep an eye out to see if they did or not. I wasn't sure it mattered. After all, they still had those walkies on their hips.

"Seems like we wrapped this up at a perfect time!" She practically beamed at us. She was so pleased with herself, it sent chills down my spine. She was *not* the same crazy nurse from before. She was still crazy, but on a whole different level, like she had taken some sort of Happy Pill.

"Do you two know the way to the Dining Hall?" she asked, still smiling.

"I know where it is!" The lie came out in a rush, but I couldn't risk Brian speaking. I wanted out of there before anything else could happen.

"Oh, excellent! Excellent! Off you go then." She opened the door for us, as she began humming a tune to herself.

I made sure to keep my head down. Something was decidedly different about Nurse Pamela, and I had no desire to stick around to find out what it was.

"Was the video *positively* amazing?" Counselor Emily asked snidely in greeting. She smiled her crocodile smile as she met us at the bottom of the steps.

"Yup. Bye!" I replied quickly. There was no way she was going to get me to stay a moment longer around the nurse's office. Not with Nurse Pamela acting all…well, creepier than usual.

"But…you. UGH! This is far from over!" Counselor Emily shouted as we rushed past her.

"What's her problem?" Brian asked.

"She's probably lost her mind, same as Nurse Pamela," I said absentmindedly. There was a sign post ahead that I was trying to make out. With any luck, it would have directions to the Dining Hall. Despite the rush I felt in being free again, I *did* feel a bit weak from hunger. The sooner we made it to the hall, the sooner I could eat and start plotting again.

"I bet you they're both crazy. I mean, they have to stay there and watch us every time someone gets in trouble, right?"

"Mhm," I answered, somewhat annoyed. Of all the times to start talking, Brian chose *this* moment. Not that it mattered too much, the sign did in fact have an arrow pointing to the Dining Hall. I took the lead as Brian kept talking.

"That means they listen to the video. Probably a lot I bet you that's why they're so crazy. Each time someone misbehaves, they get punished too."

"Haha, that's awesome," I said, suddenly following Brian's logic. No wonder the two were going crazy!

"I bet Wendy and I can break them before the video breaks us."

Brian gasped. "That's brilliant! But what will that accomplish exactly?"

"Not really sure," I said, frowning. "I mean, the rules need to be changed." I paused to think. "I've got it! If we can break those two, there won-ll…ahem…there *will* be fewer people left to enforce the punishment for rule breaking."

"Ooooh, that's brilliant! Can I help? I think the rules…are…"

"Limiting us?" I supplied for him.

"Yeah," Brian said appreciatively.

We reached the Dining Hall then only to find it relatively empty. There was one group of campers along with their counselor, but I didn't recognize anyone.

"Where do we sit?" Brian whispered.

I looked around. There was no way to tell where Wendy's group

would be sitting. There were ten long tables, one of which was full.
Plus, there was a slightly smaller table at the back of the room with
chairs only on one side, no doubt meant for the counselors to sit at.

"I see you two are on time, *for once*."

Teacher's cold voice startled me into jumping. I turned in time to
see him at the head of my old group. Everyone looked drained and
miserable. No one seemed to want to make eye contact. I hated to
think that they had a worse time with Teacher than either Brian or I
had with the video.

"Third table from the back, children. Take the half closest to the
patio doors," Teacher coldly ordered. In silence and at a painfully
slow pace, my former group walked around Teacher to the desig-
nated table. "You two," he said suddenly addressing the two of us,
"may join them. I would strongly suggest you mind your manners
lest you end up dining with me."

I swallowed hard. There was no way I would survive such a
stressful and no doubt boring meal with Teacher. Had he given that
threat to everyone? If he had, that would certainly have explained
their expressions. No one, not even Wendy or myself, would have
risked such a terrible punishment.

"Yes, sir," Brian said in wide-eyed panic. I merely nodded, my
throat too tight to utter a reply.

"Good." Teacher turned, as he did so his hands swung around his
sides until they were clasped in their customary position behind his
back. I hated the way I noticed that, but it was such a visual thing
that I couldn't help but watch.

Some other group came rushing in then. Kids were screaming
and yelling as they ran to their assigned tables. Clearly, they had not
seen Teacher yet or they would have been much quieter. As it was,
they earned a disapproving frown from the man before he continued
on his way to the head table.

"He scares me." Brian spoke so softly, I almost didn't hear him
over the noise of the other campers.

"Yeah," I agreed, finding my voice at last.

"Do you think you can break him too?"

I gave Brian a panicked look. *Break Teacher?* I wasn't even sure
it could be done. "Let's just meet up with our group," I said instead.

CHAPTER ELEVEN

Headcount

"You're back!" Wendy said, relieved. She looked awful, they all did really.

"What happened to you guys?" I asked, taking a seat next to her. I had to push Ike aside to do so, but he should have known better than to try sitting between the two of us. Brian knew better as he took a vacant spot further down.

"Could we maybe avoid talking about it?" Wendy asked.

She looked worn down, and while I wanted to press her for answers, I decided not to. One thing was clear. Teacher was not someone we wanted as an enemy. Too bad that was exactly what he was.

Our conversation ended abruptly as Counselor Melinda appeared at our table. She was followed by a loud group of kids who flew past her to reach whatever table they had been assigned to.

"Oh, dear," Counselor Melinda said as her eyes settled on Wendy and I. She laughed nervously. "You're part of my home group. That's...lovely." She gave us an equally nervous smile. "Well, it is what it is, I suppose! How is everyone doing? Having fun at camp?" She looked around, but no one answered. She may as well have asked the dead.

"Hmm, that well?" She laughed nervously again. "If I had to guess I'd say you've all met Teacher."

There were several groans.

"Thought as much. Well, I suppose I should check to make sure you're all here! Let's see...one...two...three..."

Wendy and I exchanged worried glances. Her concerned look, followed by a hasty shake of her head, confirmed my fears. We weren't all here.

"...nine...ten...*ten?*" Counselor Melinda stopped and looked around. "There should be twelve of you. Where are the other two? *Does everyone have the correct number of campers?"* Melinda shouted. Several other Counselors stood up and counted their kids while a few at the head table gave a thumbs up. Soon, Melinda had confirmation from all the other counselors.

"Everyone's here," Counselor Emily said, walking up to our table. Counselor Melinda was getting more and more agitated by the second, and I was starting to worry about Kayla being found out.

"I'm missing two," Melinda said harshly. "I've counted and re-counted. I should have twelve. Ten is…I should have twelve!"

"Ok, ok! I'll count, too."

We were counted again, despite how terribly obvious it should have looked that we only had ten. Even if we did share the table with another group, our halves were clearly marked by a gap.

"Ok," Emily said, coming to the end of her count. "Who here knows where the missing kids are?"

"They're missing?"

I wanted to warn Counselor Melinda to stop yelling, but it was too late. Teacher had heard her.

"Is there a problem, ladies?" Teacher asked as he approached our table.

"Count them!" Melinda demanded.

Teacher narrowed his eyes at her tone but counted us anyway. "There are ten of them, an even number. How many are missing?"

"Two."

"They know where they are," Emily argued suddenly, "but they refuse to say anything!"

"I've been trying to tell you we're all here-" Wendy began, acting as innocent as could be. It was at least a good start for a distraction, but I had no idea what she could possibly have hoped to accomplish.

"You've done n–"

"Careful Mrs. Emily," Teacher warned, cutting her off in time. "It is best to keep your calm when dealing with children."

"There they are," Melinda exclaimed in relief. We all looked in the direction she was facing.

Coming down the hallway at the back of the large room, and totally oblivious to the confusion they'd caused, was Kayla and Abigail.

"Where have *you* two been?" Emily demanded, her shout easily carrying down the hallway. The Dining Hall went deathly quiet, so quiet, we could all hear Abigail sniffle. It didn't take long for the shy girl to start crying.

"Enough of that!" Emily shouted at the poor girl.

"Mrs. Emily," Teacher's words came out like a hiss of acid. I know I wasn't the only one to cringe away from him. "It is clear to me, as it should be to you as well, that those two are returning from the restroom. May I suggest you keep a proper eye on them next time. Perhaps then, such situations could be *avoided*," Teacher warned. He scowled disapprovingly at Emily before settling into his customary pose with his hands clasped behind his back.

Emily sneered at his back while Melinda counted and recounted the group, her broad smile clearly showing her relief, a relief that not even Teacher's foul mood could dent.

It was a tense moment for everyone else as we all tried to keep from looking around or congratulating Wendy on her clever delaying tactic. She almost had Counselor Emily, too! Of course, she had potentially dug her own grave with Teacher.

"I'm so glad you girls are safe," Melinda said warmly as Kayla and Abigail made it to the table.

"Tsch," Emily sneered. A look from Melinda silenced her far better than anything Teacher had said or done. Counselor Emily didn't say a word as she left for the head table where the other counselors were already beginning their lunch.

"Alright, now that we are all here, you may go stand in line," Melinda said, smiling sincerely at having us all safe and accounted for.

At that moment, I didn't dislike her. I could tell Wendy had a similar change of opinion as our eyes met and she shrugged. Still, Melinda was a counselor, and that made her an enemy. If it could be helped, I decided to try and give her the *least* amount of grief. If it could be helped.

Then it dawned on me. If Kayla and Abigail had been the two absent ones, then who was the mystery camper? Kayla had rejoined the group and none of us had been any the wiser for it, so had the other camper rejoined his or her original group? Or were they part of ours? Or had they swapped with one of ours?

There was no time to ask questions as everyone began standing and heading for the long buffet line. My stomach growled, reminding me of my own hunger. Any questions I had could wait until *after* lunch.

PART TWO

Afternoon

CHAPTER TWELVE

Lunch Announcements

"May I have your attention, please."

The call startled us all, some more than others. I turned around from the lunch line in time to see some kid's soup bowl strike the ground. Luckily, there was no soup in it, but that only made the bowl clatter around more before it started awkwardly rolling. The sound certainly silenced everyone better than the call to attention had. I had to give the kid credit for letting it roll rather than chasing it down. With so many of us in line, I wasn't even sure who had dropped it.

"Thank you." The voice belonged to Mr. Petrel. As the bowl came to a stop, he gave our group a level look before turning to address the bulk of the campers who were already back at their tables and eating.

"As you may already know, several new words have been added to the list outside of camp. After lunch, we would customarily send you to the cabins for an hour of rest, however," he paused as though judging how captivated his audience was. "However, I think it wise you all become familiar with the sign and the new words. Therefore, each Counselor will take their campers to the boards outside of camp so that everyone might observe the changes."

There were several groans, and not all of them came from the campers.

"Furthermore!" The word brought silence back to the hall. "The verb *to know* will also be added, but only in its present tense. To avoid confusion, it is suggested the word be replaced with *to understand*. Is that understood, campers?" There were a few weak replies, so he asked again.

"Yes!" we shouted in reply.

"Very good. Lastly, our dear psychiatrist, Pamela, has fallen ill and has retired early for the day."

I shook my head at the latest announcement. Not only did I not believe that she had fallen ill, but Mr. Petrel had called her Psychiatrist Pamela instead of Nurse Pam. Could no one be consistent at this camp?

"As such, all disruptive campers will be sent to Teacher. That is all for this afternoon's announcements." Mr. Petrel nodded at the seated campers and then the counselors before leaving the Dining Hall.

The moment the door closed, the hall erupted in noise as everyone rushed to talk first. I immediately turned back around as I focused on getting as much food as possible so I wouldn't have to get up again.

"Did you notice everyone was staring at us?" Wendy asked in a harsh whisper as she made it back to the table and sat beside me. I was going to respond, but she kept talking. So, I picked up my dinner roll instead.

"First, when Teacher came over here, then with the bowl, but especially when Mr. Petrel called us out... Well?"

"Hm?" I asked, my mouth full of roll.

Wendy sighed. "Did you notice people staring at us?"

"I swallowed as I fought to give an answer. "Nooo-tably...so?" I frowned as I tried remembering if *notably* was a word. It seemed to fit with *so*, but Wendy had an unreadable expression that made me doubt myself, and I had felt so clever too for finding a way around my initial error of saying no.

"Mhm. Well," she continued, "they were."

"Makes sense," I said, taking another bite of my roll.

"You're just going to keep eating?" Wendy glared at me then.

I kept chewing. I didn't want her mad at me, but I didn't know what else to do. We could talk *and* eat, after all. So, why shouldn't I keep eating? Besides, it was the Dining Hall after all. I felt obliged to answer, so I shrugged to show my confusion and finished off my dinner roll.

"Ugh!"

"You ought to keep your voice down or Teacher'll come back," Kayla warned as she sat down across from us. She was closely followed by Abigail.

"Kayla! Finally, *someone* sensible to talk to," Wendy said.

"Hmph!" My protest came out muffled as I had already started on my second dinner roll. Besides, how was Kayla, the girl who had wandered off *alone* suddenly the sensible one?

Wendy ignored me. So did Kayla.

"Thanks!" Kayla practically beamed at Wendy.

"You have to tell us what you did while you were gone," Wendy pressed. Several of us leaned in as Kayla began.

"You'll nev-ugh!"

"Hahaha, I kn-" Wendy suddenly took on a serious expression as she too almost said a forbidden word. "I *understand*," she said instead with a wink.

The two girls burst out laughing.

"What's so funny?" Abigail asked.

"I'll explain later," Kayla said, wiping tears from her eyes.

"Oh, ok." Abigail said softly. She gave a quick smile before staring at her plate of food.

"It's a bit complicated with the limited speech, is all," Kayla rushed to explain.

"Oh! All right," Abigail said, smiling sincerely this time.

"Oh, please tell us what you were up to already!" Wendy begged.

More faces turned to listen in as Kayla began again.

"Well, I went around the tower and quickly found a trail. There's so much overgrowth on the trails I could barely see you guys. Anyways, that's where I met Tyler."

"Yo," Tyler said, tilting his head so we'd all know who he was.

Kayla giggled. "He's awesome, right? Anyway, Tyler saw me sneak out of the group and he followed. He used to go here, back when this camp belonged to Mr. McGregor. There's a ton of cool stuff back there that I doubt even the adults know about."

"We may be able to use that…" Wendy said.

"Yeah, but the adults're keeping an awfully close eye on us," someone else noted.

"Good," Wendy said with her awesomely wicked grin. "They'll be too focused on us to pay attention to the other groups."

"What do you mean?" I asked, curious to know what Wendy had been up to while we had been separated.

"But what's back there?" Brian asked.

Wendy gave me a conspiratory wink, but then turned her attention back to the conversation.

"They had a rope course back there," Tyler said, taking charge. "The old camp used it for races or sometimes for team building exercises."

"Exactly," Kayla continued, cutting Tyler off in her excitement. "And that's where I found Tyler."

"I thought he followed after you?" I asked.

"Where did your food go?" Wendy asked in shock. She must have realized I had stopped talking with my mouth full.

"I ate it?"

"Nah, I snuck off just before Kayla did," Tyler said, ignoring us. "I knew the old trails, so I figured I could sneak back before Coach noticed."

"That's so cool!" Wendy said, apparently completely over my empty plate.

"Did they have anything we could use?" I asked.

"What do you mean?" Kayla asked.

I looked at Kayla, my mind blank. I had only asked to get Wendy's attention back on me and away from perfect Tyler.

"Good idea," Wendy said, unintentionally coming to my aid. "We could really use some help in tripping the counselors up. We've been using words to break the rules, but they just make them forbidden. Eventually, we'll run out of words. So, how else can we trip them up? Make them break their own rules and see how ridiculous they are?"

"Does the old camp have any traps?" I asked lamely.

"There's an old mud trail," Tyler said slowly, "people used to lose shoes and things in the mud all the time. Would that work?"

"Is it avoidable? Could they just walk around?" Kayla asked as she rejoined the conversation.

"Yeah, they could. The mud is pretty obvious," Tyler said, frowning.

"What about the old trails?" Brian asked. His voice made us all look around cautiously.

"Keep your voice down," Wendy warned. "Now what do you mean?"

"Where else do they go?"

"We followed one to the art barn," Kayla said. "We saw you out back, Wendy..."

"Oh," Wendy said slowly. "Then you saw?"

"I'd have screamed too," Kayla said comfortingly.

"Why did you scream? What did he do?" I asked, furious for leaving Wendy behind.

She laughed uneasily.

"The back of the barn is covered with spider webs," Kayla said slowly.

"Not just webs," Wendy replied with a shiver.

"Poisonous ones?" Abigail asked, her eyes wide with fear.

"I tried not to look. I screamed because I thought one jumped on me. Then something moved in the bushes..."

"Sorry," Kayla apologized. "I wanted to help, but then that Teacher guy came out."

"Yeah." Wendy shivered again.

"Wait," I said, an idea forming. "The trail led to the barn?" If it led to the barn, then there was the possibility of doing some sort of sneak attack on Teacher. I wasn't sure how to strike back, so I let the idea slip as Kayla started talking again.

"Not sure how that helps anything, but-" Kayla was cut off as Abigail shushed her.

"I see you found your way back to the group, Daniel."

I didn't have to turn around to know that it was Teacher who had spoken from behind me. I turned around anyway, since he was talking to me.

"I thought I had made it clear that you and miss Wendy were to be separated. This shall be remedied right now. You and the camper you were with earlier are to join Dave's Home Group until further notice. I'm sure you are familiar with Counselor Dave?"

"Yes, sir." I decided not to argue. What would be the point? Besides, I still had that vengeful idea running through my mind, distracting me.

"Then move."

Brian bolted at the command. I moved quickly, but not as quickly as I could have. Spiders didn't scare me, and besides, I had an idea on how to take care of creepy ol' Teacher.

CHAPTER THIRTEEN

The Message

"Welcome back to the group, Camper Daniel!" Dave shouted cheerfully, a wide smile on his face.

Counselor Dave looked as excited as he sounded, something that made my skin crawl. How could he forget so quickly what Wendy and I had done to him? Or forgive?

"Hello, Counselor Dave," Brian said glumly.

"Hello, camper! Welcome to our group! You can call me Davy. What's your name?"

I tried to keep my face blank, but the way he had said *Davy* made me regret eating so much food. From the looks on his campers' faces, I wasn't the only one disturbed by the guy.

"Brian," Brian said hesitantly. I didn't blame him one bit.

"B for brave! R for righteous! I for integrity! A for astounding! N for night! It's nice to meet you, Knightly Brian!"

My jaw dropped in disbelief. Mr. Chipper, as I still found myself thinking of him, was more sickly sweet and outgoing than I remembered him being. At that moment, I wanted to cry. Spending time with Teacher felt preferable than spending time with *Davy*.

"Well, my happy troop! Let's head off to the signs out front and read those words. Then it's off to your Home Cabins for a quick siiiiiiiiesta!"

"What's a siesta?" a foolish camper asked.

I was more interested in what he meant by *Home Cabin*, but I kept my mouth shut. Talking with *Davy* hurt my head too much.

"A siesta is a form of rest, like a nap. It's often done after lunch as that is the hottest part of the day; however, today we are taking it early so you campers can get adjusted to our schedule. Is that swell, or what?" He pumped his arm to emphasize his cheer.

"Or what," I said too quietly for Mr. Chipper to hear me. Brian gave a little laugh, but I couldn't tell if it was a nervous laugh, completely understandable given what he had just gone through, or if he'd heard me.

"Form a line, my troop of cheer!"

There were a few groans from the group, which gave me some hope. *They*, at least, were normal if they found Dave abnormally cheerful. "Daniel, you and Brian can be at the head of the line today. Everyone gets a chance to be first at least once in *my* troop."

Brian and I reluctantly made our way to the front of the line. I had a sinking suspicion we were going to be at the front a lot, or at the very least, I was going to be.

"We're off to the signs!" Dave announced as we finished forming our less than chipper line.

No one talked as we made the dreadful walk. We saw other groups making the same journey, but somehow, they were all spaced enough apart to keep campers secluded and stuck in their own groups. It seemed too perfect to have been an accident.

Before we had gone too far, Brian jabbed me in the back. His nail dug in painfully between a muscle or something and the pain took me completely by surprise. As I cried out, Brian stuffed something into my hand faster than Counselor Dave could turn around.

"Is everything alright, camper?" Dave waved everyone to a stop as he addressed me.

"Yeah," I lied, but my tone came out harsher than I had intended.

Dave gave me a faintly suspicious look, one I barely noticed since he still had that goofy smile on his face. He leaned down, and I panicked. Acting quickly, I rubbed my arm, careful to keep the paper Brian had given me concealed. I pinched a spot for good measure, hoping I could pass that off as being the source of my pain rather than the sore spot on my back where Brian had jabbed me.

"Bug bit me," I lied. I pretended to inspect the pinched area, and Dave backed away.

"Careful of the Horseflies around here, my happy troop! Their bites can be painful." He turned around, and we began moving again.

I didn't dare open the paper, not with *Davy* looking back every so often now. I cursed my rotten luck. He hadn't started randomly looking back until after I had shouted. It didn't matter, they couldn't watch me forever.

Then an idea hit me. I quickly cupped my hand around the spot I had pinched myself. With my eyes on Dave, I carefully opened my hand enough to read the message, all the while keeping it cupped around the fake bug bite.

Want 2 help. How? the paper read.

I closed my hand over my arm and focused on keeping my expression blank. If only I had a pencil or something! But how was I supposed to write a complex plan on a tiny piece of paper? And I wasn't even sure I *had* a plan. Not yet, anyway.

I used the rest of the time thinking of something that could be done and how to say it in only a few words. When I had the words in my mind, I repeated them over and over, fearful I would forget before I could write the message down.

We reached the signs outside of camp shortly after that. Dave said some things, but I didn't listen. I was too busy trying to remember my message. He certainly talked for a while. There was something about being good, doing good, and a whole bunch of nonsense that I would have wanted to block out anyway.

Then it came. As we were all clustered around the signs, no longer trapped in a solitary line, someone stabbed me with what felt like a pencil tip. I took it, hopeful that they hadn't broken the tip of it off on my arm. What was it with everyone stabbing me, anyway?

Suddenly the area in front of me became overly crowded as campers nudged each other and pushed each other as they formed a wall in front of me.

"What are you doing? Chelsea, speak up, please."

Dave had noticed all the movement! I froze, my hands already in position for me to write my message on the back of the paper.

"Macey's in my spot!" Chelsea cried indignantly.

"It's *my* spot," Macey retorted.

"Girls, girls! We must share our space." Dave tried in vain to settle the argument, but it was clear he was struggling to find the *positive* words to do so.

I didn't care if the argument was a ruse or not, I used it and quickly jotted down my message. *Do opposite of rules.*

I passed the message to the nearest camper. He gave me a brief nod as he accepted and carefully hid the paper. In that moment, I knew a resistance had been formed.

CHAPTER FOURTEEN

The Argument

"Alright, Campers! We're off to the cabins for a siesta!" Dave announced suddenly, no doubt as he fought to stay in charge.

"But Macey's in my spot!" Chelsea continued to argue.

"It's mine!" Macey retorted.

"Why are you letting her get away with this?" Chelsea turned on Dave.

Dave had been about to speak, but the question took him completely off guard. "Uh, let's form a line, campers." His voice lacked sufficient command to make anyone move, and I noted that he sounded far less chipper than usual.

"You *are* taking her side," Chelsea whined.

"Ha! I told you this is *my* spot."

"Ladies. Ladies, please!"

"What? You're switching to *her* side now?" Macey stomped her foot angrily.

"Ha! It's only fair. I'm the one who's right."

"LADIES!"

Chipper Dave was crumbling beautifully, and I wasn't even doing anything.

"What?" they demanded in unison.

"Mrs. Parker will settle the debate back at the cabins," Dave informed them calmly.

I frowned. It figured he would find a way to shift the task to someone else. That wasn't fair. I decided to join in on the fun. Unfortunately, Dave cut me off before I could.

"Please, campers. Get in line so we can have some super-awe-some-fun siesta time!"

Dave's cheerfulness was returning, I had to act fast! "How are they supposed to get in line when their spots are mixed up?" I asked as innocently as I could.

"Yeah! And how come the new kid gets to be first in line?" one of the guys chimed in.

"Campers..." Dave began.

"Wait, why *is* he first?"

"...spots are..."

"He took my spot!"

"...liable to change." Dave could barely be heard over the sudden uproar or protest.

"You said the number one spot was for good campers!"

"Yeah, and that other kid took mine, too!"

"I thought I was your number one?" a new voice moaned piteously.

"Where am I supposed to go again?" some goody-goody-two-shoes asked, sounding sincerely concerned. He and I were going to have a *talk* later. There could be no sympathy in the resistance!

Someone started crying.

"You made Michelle cry."

"Well, Chelsea pushed me into her. It's *her* fault."

"Campers ..."

"You pushed me first!"

"...pushing..."

"She should have dodged!"

"...is forbidden. Campers?"

"That does it! You're both getting pushed!"

"Campers! Get in a line, NOW!"

Chipper Dave died that day. The best part though, the poor guy didn't even know how bad he had it. Not until a new voice joined the fray.

"Counselor, Dave. What seems to be the matter here?"

The look of pure terror as Dave heard Mr. Petrel's voice was almost enough to make me sorry for him.

"Uh... Mr. Petrel. You see...uh."

"Yes, I can see you have your hands full. Perhaps it would be best if you took a break in the Nurse's Station."

"Oh, well. Sir, really. I'm alright."

"Are you? You seem tired. Go and rest up." Mr. Petrel guided Dave away from our deathly silent group.

"Now children," he said, turning back to us as dazed Dave kept walking. "I shall be accompanying you to your cabins. If you could form two lines, one with the ladies and the other with the gentlemen."

"In what order?" a brave soul asked.

"In any order," the coldness of the words silenced any further objections.

It took me a moment to realize it, but there was silence all around. I looked around for the person who had been crying, Michelle or something, but there was just silence. Well, silence and obedience. We were all quietly forming our lines.

"Very good, children. Now then, let's keep this atmosphere as we make our way to the cabins. If we hurry, you may even have time for a proper siesta. Is that understood?"

There were varying affirmative replies. Luckily, he didn't make any of us repeat our lackluster responses.

"Excellent. Off we go then."

I paused to look back at the words etched on the boards outside of camp. There were more signs now, I noted with a barely concealed grin. As I passed under the signs, I committed the new and the old to memory.

No, not and any contraction thereof, the prefix un-, less than, bad, nasty, awful, terrible, worse, hate, worthless, never, cusswords of any kind, derogatory words such as dumb, stupid, idiot, etc.

defective, abhorrent, vile, egregious, wicked, execrable, negativity, deplorable, ya-hoo, disturbed, annoyed, naughty, indifferent, embattled, loathe

troublesome, bitter, negative, disappointed, wrong

The verb "to know" - in its present tense - shall be replaced by the verb "to understand"

CHAPTER FIFTEEN

Siesta with Markus

When we reached the bathhouse, Mr. Petrel sent the girls down a different path. The girls broke up into smaller groups as they went to the Home Cabin they had been assigned to. Before I could dwell on the significance of that, Mr. Petrel took us down a path to our own cabins. Then we too were separating into our own respective buildings.

Up until that moment, I had no idea who shared a cabin with me. No one in any of my groups had said anything about belonging to *House Joy*, and I didn't blame them. I was alone as I walked to my cabin. As I passed under the sign with the cabin's name on it, I couldn't help resenting it. If I had to stay at a camp this stupid, I at least figured they would have better names for their buildings.

With my eyes focused on the ridiculous name, I noticed something odd about the sign. Before I could be caught gawking, I rushed inside. Worried my expression might give me away, I focused on my anger, which wasn't difficult as the cabin name really had me irked.

"Welcome, Camper," someone said quietly from somewhere in the dark recesses of the cabin. "Please make your way to your bunk. There are forty-seven minutes left of our siesta. You may nap if you like, we just ask that you stay quiet."

"Ok." I was immediately shushed, but I didn't care. My mind was too focused on the newest discovery to care about that.

I kicked off my shoes and collapsed on the rolled out sleeping bag on my bed. My thoughts were too chaotic for me to have more than a few seconds of envy for the person who had claimed the top bunk. There were so many things to think about! I barely even registered that someone else walked into the cabin.

The bright light illuminated the space long enough for me to make out the carved names and messages on the wooden board above my bed. I stared at it, my mind too awake and too strung out to make out anything useful.

I sighed and closed my eyes. I needed to calm down, to think, to formulate a plan. After a few calming breaths, I was able to think clearly again. My thoughts immediately went back to the most recent thing I had seen, the cabin name.

The sign for *House Joy* had been *hung* on the building, and it had the same style of writing as the signs outside of camp. That wasn't even the best part! I had seen a board behind the false sign. It had to be a name plaque. If given the chance, I was going to find a way to tear the fake name down. Anything sounded better than *House Joy*.

Someone's bed creaked and the unknown counselor, at least to me since I hadn't paid attention earlier that morning, asked us to remain quiet. The sound drew me out of my thoughts and sent me on a whole new tangent.

Even if everyone kept using words with *negative* meanings, eventually we would run out of words to use. True, we only had three days, but then some other group of campers would be stuck with our revised list. Who knew how long a resistance like that could survive. Something else had to be done. The camp had to be shut down, not changed.

A resistance.

There were others invested in the cause now. I looked around the cabin. Without the lights on, it was difficult to make out many details. There were curtains over the windows too, no doubt to help us have a *restful* siesta. Someone was writing a letter to their parents, at least it looked like that was what they were doing.

A letter? We could write during a siesta! That meant we could pass more messages along, ones more elaborate than a few words, too. I didn't have any paper with me, or at least not any that was easily accessible. I didn't feel like being shushed again for rifling through my stuff.

Still, there was hope! Now we just had to be able to communicate and act as a group. Then it hit me, the girls had all gone off to the girls' cabins, but like us, they had split off further as they went to a specific one.

"Bingo," I said softly as yet one more thing clicked into place.

"Quiet, please," the counselor warned me softly.

I scowled at the guy for a moment, but then my eyes met a familiar face. The kid winked and I grinned. Before anyone could notice the exchange, I went back to staring at the bottom of the bed above me.

We had our method of communication, a way to disperse and spread the news to everyone, time to do it, and Tyler, our expert on the layout of the camp, was in my cabin. The counselors didn't stand a chance!

Now all we had to do was cause enough chaos for me to initiate my vengeful plan against Teacher, and I had plenty of time to think of a way to do just that.

CHAPTER SIXTEEN

The Plan

Rest hour dragged on painfully. I had my plan more or less worked out already. I just needed to wait for nightfall, sneak out of the cabin with a false bathroom break, make my way to the Art Barn, and destroy or hide all of Teacher's wood plaques. Without those, he wouldn't be able to make more of those stupid forbidding signs.

Phase two involved causing problems at breakfast. If there was one thing I had learned from school, it was that motivated kids woke up faster and far more energized than adults. With all the constraints they put on us, I had little doubt that the resistance would be strong. Without the ability to make more signs, and being less than awake, there was no way the counselors could keep up with us!

Phase three, while equally epic, was more of a wish list than an actual plan. It involved taking back the camp and returning it to its former fun filled glory. The signs above the cabins had to go, then there was the climbing rock tower, and who knew what else there was to reclaim? The rope course Kayla or Tyler had mentioned? What about the kayaks and canoes by the beach?

Still, rest hour dragged on. Even our counselor felt the time lag as he kept looking at his watch and tapping his foot. I thought about pulling my phone out, but my parents had taken it away before ditching me. Wendy still had hers, I remembered then. However, that did little to help me relieve my boredom now.

Laying there, I wondered what was next on the schedule. The whole camp was rather confusing. We each had our own Home Cabin, but then we had a Home Group we met with in the morning and stayed with for the day. I'd have argued against that, but then I never would have met Wendy, or any of the girls for that matter.

As I stared at the etchings above me, I suddenly remembered the schedule in my pocket. I pulled out the paper and rolled over as I tried finding the right angle so I could read it in the dim light.

Day 1
Group C Schedule

7-7:50	*Settling in*
8-8:50	*Counselor Dave – Team building / Camp Introduction / Sorting*
9-9:50	*Counselor Melinda (Home Group) – Music*
10-10:50	*Counselor (Coach) Tammy – Field Games*
11-11:50	*Counselor Teacher – Art Barn*
12-1	*Lunch*
1-2	*Rest Hour – House Joy (Home Cabin)*
2-2:50	*Counselor Markus – House Joy & Camp Cleanup Counselor*
3-3:50	*Counselor Nathan – Creature Feature*
4-4:50	*Counselor Delilah – Stress Relief / Yoga*
5-6	*Dinner*
6-6:50	*Counselor Kimberly – Nature Walk*
7-7:50	*Campfire Stories*
8-8:50	*Counselor Lenel & Counselor Melinda – Campfire Songs*
9	*Lights Out*
9-8am	*Sleep*

When my eyes came to Teacher's title, I snickered to myself. The sound awarded me another warning from – I looked at my schedule and found his name – Counselor Markus. Apparently, his schedule remained the same for me too. From the look of it, he would also be our *Camp Cleanup Counselor*. I hated to think what that activity would entail.

"Looks like I get to find out," I grumbled as a twinkling sound, no doubt some positively cheerful alarm, went off on Counselor Markus' nightstand. Rest hour was over.

CHAPTER SEVENTEEN

Camp Cleanup with Markus

"Alright, House Joy. Before you go running off to join up with your Home Group, we are heading to the beach for our next camp activity."

I shook my head at the cries of excitement. If I hadn't read the schedule, I probably would have been excited as well, but I knew better. We weren't going to the beach for fun, we were going there to work on *Camp Cleanup*.

"Do we get to go swimming now?" "Should we change?" "We have a *beach?*" Everyone kept shouting out questions, but Counselor Markus quickly took charge.

"Sorry, kiddos. Swimming can only be done with a lifeguard, and Positivity Camp is currently without one. We're going down to the beach for Camp Cleanup!"

"For *what?*" someone groaned.

Luckily for them, Counselor Markus struggled to pinpoint who had spoken, and before he could take control of the situation, there were several more groans followed by more whining.

"Knock it off, crybabies."

And surprise, surprise the camp bully emerged from the darkness that was House Joy. Unfortunately, I did see his point. Now that we were outside, I saw again the difference in age ranges within the group. I was among the older kids, which was so much different than the group with Wendy which had similar age ranges. Still, younger kids could be annoying. They proved the point by whining and complaining further.

"Mitchel!" Counselor Markus shouted over the arguments that had broken out.

"Sorry, Counselor Markus."

"Apologize to–"

"But maybe if there were fewer babies, I'd be better behaved. Just swap out a baby or two with an older kid from another cabin."

As much as I hated to hear Mitchel talk about the younger kids like that, I also understood his point. The whining and arguing stopped, however, as Counselor Markus silenced them with a look before turning his attention back to Mitchel.

"Mitchel, to the nurses' station for the use of demeaning language. Now!" he added as Mitchel remained unmoving.

"Look, just move me to a different cabin," Mitchel argued.

"All cabins are arranged this way so that all campers might experience and grow together."

A sudden change came over our counselor as he spoke of *growing together.* He became calmer and surer of himself, despite Mitchel's outburst. We all grew quiet as he continued spouting Positivity Camp doctrines.

Counselor Markus opened his arms wide as he spoke, "The schedules you each received put you into a similar age range, but we find it important to foster positive relationships with *all* ages. Think of it as a *learning experience*." Then he looked at Mitchel and his face became devoid of joy or anger. "That means *any* cabin you go to will have a range of ages. Is that understood campers?"

"Yes, Counselor Markus!" We all shouted, even Mitchel. I could tell he hated saying it as much as I had. The odd behavior had put me on edge, and I had responded without intending to. What was this camp doing to us?

"Good, now what's your name?" Counselor Markus asked of one of the older kids standing near Mitchel.

"Jackal."

"Jackal?" The counselor gave him a long hard look before seeming to accept the name.

"Yes," Jackal said after a long and awkward silence.

"Right." Counselor Markus looked uncomfortable for a moment. "Jackal, you are to take Mitchel to the nurses' office."

"Why there?"

"Why? Because he needs a refresher on what this camp stands for."

"Yes, but why the nurse?"

"Because Psychiatrist Pam will have him watch the Positivity Camp video."

"Why there then?"

"I just said why, now please get going."

It was clear to everyone that Counselor Markus was losing his patience, but I couldn't blame him. I saw both sides of the issue. Nurse Pam or Psychiatrist Pamela had gone home for the day. So, Jackal wasn't entirely wrong in pointing that out. However, he was doing a terrible job of it. I couldn't blame him though. It was difficult to say the woman wasn't there when that sort of language involved *negative* words. The confusion caused by the breakdown in communication was beautiful to behold!

"But is she there?"

"It's the nurses' station, of course she's there." Counselor Markus was doing his best to keep a smile on his face, but he was clearly breaking.

"Is she though?"

"Jackal, one more word, and I'll send you both to Teacher."

"Counselor Markus," cool kid Tyler spoke up. I still disliked him for ditching us with Coach Tammy and for the way the girls reacted around him. "Nurse Pamela was sent home for the day."

"That's what I've been saying!" Jackal said with a glare at the counselor.

"She… Oh, right. She was sent home. Sorry, Jackal. You two are to head to Teacher then at the Art Barn. He'll be the one to instruct you in the ways of Positivity Camp. Besides, he'll need to make a new sign anyway."

"An infantile one," Mitchel said straight faced as he brushed past the now fuming counselor.

"OFF WITH YOU!"

"I was already going," Mitchel called back.

As the two of them walked by me, Mitchel shot me a wink, and I was pretty certain I saw Jackal suppressing a laugh. I did my best to keep my features blank. Suddenly the outburst made more sense. The resistance was striking back! Though, I did worry it was doing so in a bad way. I hoped the younger kids knew Mitchel wasn't being mean intentionally.

"Let's bring that cheer back and head down to the waterfront!" Counselor Markus called out in a disturbingly happy way. His face no longer held the quiet rage from before, but it also looked inhumanly happy.

There was no cheer as the remainder of us made our way to the waterfront. Counselor Markus ignored us most of the way as he radioed Teacher to let him know what had happened.

"Hey. Psssst. Hey. Pssssssssssst!"

I turned and saw Tyler coming up beside me. I wasn't exactly sure how I felt about that. He had that laid back, casual air about him that I didn't like.

"What do you want?" I asked, the question coming across harsher than I had intended. "Counselor Markus is already on edge."

"Yeah, yeah," Tyler said, giving a dismissive wave of his hand. The action only added to my aggravation. "Listen, find me during clean up. I have a way to sneak kids out of camp."

"What did you just say?" I asked, shocked.

"Find me during clean up," he answered elusively.

Before I could question him further on his crazy scheme, he darted back to a small cluster of kids. My mind was whirling with questions, concerns, and revised schemes even as we made our way down the giant stone steps leading to the waterfront.

CHAPTER EIGHTEEN

Tyler's Plan

All thoughts of Tyler and his crazy scheme vanished as we arrived at the waterfront. There were shouts of joy as our group ran for the beach. Before Counselor Markus caught up, several of us, myself included, had our shoes off and our feet in the sand.

The sand quickly shifted from warm and welcoming to a burning fire beneath my feet. I burrowed them down into the sand further until I found a more reasonable temperature. When I looked up, I saw other kids dancing around like fools while others retreated to their shoes.

"Amateurs."

"The sand is hot, children," Counselor Markus warned a tad too late.

"Hey, how come the boats are locked up?" a kid asked as he stepped away from the shadowy side of the beach shed.

I had seen the canoes from the hilltop earlier. They had been flipped over on some giant metal rack, but I couldn't see them now that I was on the same level with them. For some reason, his question confused me, but before I could figure out why, someone else shifted the topic to the nearby shed.

"Who cares about the boats! What's in there?"

"When did you find the boats?" Counselor Markus asked, completely ignoring the question about the shed. "Those canoes are way past the shed on the other end of the beach near the old dock."

Now that he said it, I realized what had been bothering me about the kid. He wasn't panting, and from what I remembered, the boats *had* been a long way down the beach. So, how had the kid made it down there, discovered the locks, made it back again without anyone having noticed, *and* managed not to get winded?

Much to my dismay, and no doubt Counselor Markus' as well, the kid merely stood there and shrugged. No one else seemed to care. In fact, someone else immediately jumped into bombarding the counselor with questions. At that point, I decided to let it go. This camp was too odd for me to waste time on why there would be locks on boats.

"There's an old dock?!" the kid began. Without missing a beat, he jumped into his next question, and then the next and the next. I wasn't even sure he was breathing. "Where is it? Is it for fishing? Can we go fishing? Are lifeguards needed for fishing? Wait!! Lifeguards are for swimming! So, we *can* go fishing! Right? When though? When can we go fishing? Is the shack full of fishing gear? Do we need to collect our own worms? Is there dry bait?"

To his credit, Counselor Markus tried only once to break in and either stop or answer the questions. After that, he gave up, and while the kid kept talking, he ordered the rest of us to grab a bag from the sack he carried and pick up any trash we saw on this side of the waterfront fence. Then he calmly, if defeatedly, went back to listening as the kid seamlessly shifted to questioning him about the types of fish he could hope to catch.

I shook my head as I took my bag. One thing was certain, no one wanted that kid following them around asking questions. In an unspoken agreement, we all scattered, leaving Counselor Markus alone with the unending stream of questions.

"I swear," Tyler said, sneaking up beside me, "every camp has one."

"Has one what?" I asked, falling for the bait.

"A Million Questions Kid."

I grunted in response. For some reason, Tyler really bugged me. Even though I was curious to learn more of his plan, I couldn't bring myself to ask the question. The silence grew between us, but I refused to give in.

"So," he spoke up at last, acting cool and unaffected by the silent treatment. "Now that we're alone, what do you think of my plan?"

I looked around to see if we were actually alone. There were others around, but they were too far to hear us. "What plan?" I asked while still keeping an eye out.

"The one to sneak everyone out of camp!" Despite his excitement, Tyler did manage to keep his voice down.

"I'd hardly call that a plan."

"Ha! Fair enough. Still interested though?"

"I think I am? I mean, it sounds interesting, but how would we do it? And where would everyone go? It sounds dangerous."

"Hmm, those are good questions," Tyler said slowly.

"Yes, they are," I added dryly. I wasn't liking Tyler's laid back attitude about such a risky plan.

"Ha! I like your style, Daniel. Together, I think we could really pull this off."

I tried not to show my lack of enthusiasm.

"The how is simple. Well, simple to explain anyway."

"Alright," I said simply.

"Tonight while the counselors sleep, we – we being each cabin – sneak out, meet at a specific path in the woods, and leave camp. This works best in small groups, so we'd want to go cabin by cabin."

"Alright," I said, this time with more enthusiasm, but not much.

"Then I lead each group outside of camp and take them to my house. My parents are away so the place'll be empty."

"Do you live near here?"

"Yeah, about a thirty-minute walk down some old trails."

"Well, that answers the how and the where."

"Are we doing it then?"

"Hold on," I said with a quick shake of my head. "It's a...alright plan, but I'm..." I paused as I tried to use positive words. "I mean, how is this going to...hmm...stop the camp? It's great for our group, but what about future campers? And *can* we sneak everyone out in one night?"

"Hmm. Well, I'm pretty sure the camp would close if word got out that kids went missing."

"True," I said thoughtfully, but I still wasn't convinced we could sneak everyone out. "Would we need to get everyone out?"

"Maybe you're right. Maybe only a cabin or two need to go missing."

"That's true," I agreed, still feeling a little skeptical and unenthused about having Tyler as a co-conspirator. Still, the plan did have some merit to it.

"See! I told you we would make a great team!"

I cringed internally. "If this is going to work, we'll need a more solid plan. We'll also want to spread the word."

"We have an hour," Tyler reminded me. "And that kid is keeping Counselor Markus busy." He shot the pair a mischievous grin before looking back at me. I couldn't help but smile back. Tyler was right, we had the time, no one was watching, and judging by the way a few others kept looking at us, we had plenty of volunteers. It was perfect! The counselors weren't going to know what hit them!

CHAPTER NINETEEN

The Details

"So, what exactly do you plan to do? I mean, how late are we talking here?" I asked Tyler as I tried gauging the likelihood of us pulling off his plan.

"How late for what?" Tyler asked in his infuriatingly clueless way.

"How late do we have to stay up before freeing a cabin of kids?"

"Oh, that part of the plan!"

"Quiet, you fool!" I looked around to see if anyone had noticed, but everyone looked too involved in their own group chats. No one was doing any cleaning up.

"Oh, right…"

I gave Tyler a cold look.

"So, yeah. Late. It'll be late."

"How late?"

"Um…when the counselors fall asleep? Or just Counselor Markus. That late." He gave a stupid grin as he finished talking, as though he'd given the best response ever.

I seriously began losing interest. While Tyler continued looking proud of himself, my eyes searched for the canoe kid. If anyone had anything interesting to say or do, it would be him.

"Alright, it's settled then!"

"What is?" I turned my attention hesitantly back to Tyler.

"We'll wait till late tonight, sneak out with our cabin, free some others, take the trail back to my place, and wait for the camp to close."

When had I agreed to do any of this? And why was he acting like his plan was so complete when it wasn't? He stated it all so matter-of-factly, that I wasn't able to say much more than, "Uh."

"But there's something I need you to do first. Can you tell the girls and anyone else you see? I've got to go get things ready, you know, make sure the trail is marked and stuff."

"...make sure the trail is marked?" I asked, bemused by the stupidity of the statement. "Wait, you do...uh..." I paused as I tried to think of how I could ask him if he knew the way to his house without saying *know*. My hesitation cost me.

"No! Why don't you pick it up! This is so lame!"

"What?" I took a step back as the idiot suddenly began yelling loud enough for everyone to hear.

"The counselors should be the ones picking up camp, not us!" Tyler winked and then spoke so only I could hear him, "Don't worry, I've got this." Then he winked again.

I looked around to see if anyone else understood what was going on. There were dropped jaws and wide eyes all around. Even Counselor Markus snapped to attention. It was then that I suddenly translated what Tyler had said and the negative words he'd used.

"What are you doing?" I shouted at him. How could he be so stupid as to start spouting forbidden words?

He answered with another more elaborate wink.

"What is your name?" Counselor Markus demanded as he approached us. "Those were forbidden words you just used! I would have expected such behavior from Daniel, but you..."

"Thanks," I muttered dryly.

"The name's Tyler." Tyler gave one of his *cool kid* nods.

"Well, Tyler, you've just earned yourself a visit to Counselor Pamela."

"Do you mean Nurse Pam?" the question kid chimed in. Apparently, he had followed Counselor Markus and wasn't about to let up on his million questions either. "Hey, you do remember she left for the day, right? I'm pretty sure she left anyway. She did leave, right? So how can he go see the lady if she's gone?"

"Brilliant!" Counselor Markus exclaimed suddenly.

We all stared as the poor guy finally lost it.

He cleared his throat before continuing. "Yes, I am aware she has left for the day. Thank you for reminding me, Jiminy. Would you be so good as to escort Tyler to Teacher for me?"

"Are you sure you want me to do it?"

"*Yes!* Ahem...yes. As you remember things so well, I think it best that it be you who goes."

"Fine by me," Tyler chimed in.

Counselor Markus gave him a dark look, but one sideways

glance at Jiminy had him shutting his mouth. The counselor *really* wanted Jiminy gone.

Tyler gave me his cool kid nod.

I tried keeping my expression blank so he wouldn't see how annoyed I was, but as he introduced himself to Jiminy, to which Jiminy immediately spouted off another round of questions, I gritted my teeth.

"You can talk on your way to the Art Barn," Counselor Markus said cheerfully. He grabbed Tyler by the shoulder and spun Jiminy around. He then gave both a gentle push to get them moving. Not that Tyler needed any motivation. Jiminy, however, would have likely stayed put, given a choice.

Counselor Markus checked the time and grumbled. He shot me a look, and I did my best to look busy. I failed miserably as I stared up at some tree branches.

"Trash is on the ground, Daniel," Markus reminded me with a sour look.

I would have kept my peace, but he just had to push me!

"Hey, Jiminy!" I called out. "Wait up a sec!" Jiminy stopped and turned around.

I looked at Markus. Markus looked at me. I raised an eyebrow, daring the counselor to push me. One forbidden word and there would be no need for Jiminy to escort Tyler, because I would end up taking his place. It took only a second for Counselor Markus' eyes to narrow as he understood what I was hinting at.

"Touché," he conceded with a slight nod of his head. Then he turned away and let the subject drop.

"False alarm, Jiminy!" I shouted back. I might have pressed the issue, but Jiminy would eventually be out of range, and I didn't need another counselor against me, at least not any more than he already was. Plus, I had no desire to go see Teacher again.

"Aw!"

"Sorry!" I wasn't sorry.

With Tyler gone, I decided to kill time looking more thoroughly for the canoe kid. Being as discreet as possible, I wandered around, pretending to look for trash. I kept my eyes on the ground as much as possible, but I did look up every now and again to see if I could spot the kid I was looking for.

No such luck. I debated heading over to the shack to try casually walking behind it before making my way to the other end of the beach where all the canoes were, but Counselor Markus kept staring in my direction. Most kids had wandered off, making it difficult for

me to easily join a group or to have someone distract him enough
for me to go exploring.

If it hadn't been for Tyler, I realized, I could have slipped away
sooner. With Jiminy there, any of us could have done anything. Instead, we had wasted time on a stupid plan! Well, if his plan failed,
as I suspected it would, I still had a backup plan. I could still strip
down the signs on the cabins and hide all of Teacher's signs, or maybe just hide the thing he used to make them?

Regardless, I found myself disliking Tyler more and more.

CHAPTER TWENTY

New Schedule

Counselor Markus' alarm went off before I had finished my search for the canoe kid and before I could slink off and explore the beach for the canoes. If I could have slipped away, all the trees and bushes on the other side of the shack would have shielded me from the counselor's watchful eyes. Not that it mattered; time was up.

"Alright campers! Let's regroup, Camp Cleanup is almost over!"

It took several minutes for everyone to wander back. I wasn't surprised to see the canoe kid reappear from the other side of the shack, though I did envy him.

I was a bit surprised to see Counselor Markus in such a good mood. He looked at his watch once, but showed no signs of concern, which meant he had probably set his timer sooner to give the slow-pokes a chance to make it back. That was great for him and all, but I wanted to get going!

I pulled out my paper and checked to see what was next on my schedule. There was no use getting excited if it was something lame.

Sweet! I had Creature Feature with Counselor Nathan next! Surely a camp this bad couldn't ruin something that amazing. I mean, there was a chance, but what were the odds? I mean, to go through the effort of *having* a program like that and then to *work* at ruining it? No, there had to be hope! There just *had* to be!

"What do you have there, Daniel?" Counselor Markus asked.

I took an involuntary step back as I looked up to see the counselor standing directly in front of me.

"Itismyschedule," I said in a rush.

"Your what? Ah! Your schedule. That reminds me, if anyone has any questions on where they're to go next, please ask. But first," he said as several voices interrupted, "I am to give you this." He handed me a paper.

"What is it?" I asked, but he was already walking toward one of the kids who had shouted out for help only a moment before. I unfolded the paper and looked at it.

Revised Day 1
Group F Schedule

7-7:50	*Settling in*
8-8:50	*Counselor Lev – Team building / Camp Introduction / Sorting*
9-9:50	*Counselor Delilah (Home Group) – Stress Relief / Yoga*
10-10:50	*Counselor (Coach) Tammy – Field Games*
11-11:50	*Counselor Nathan – Creature Feature*
12-1	*Lunch*
1-2	*Rest Hour – House Joy*
2-2:50	*Counselor Markus – House Joy & Camp Cleanup Counselor*
3-3:50	*Counselor Teacher – Art Barn*
4-4:50	*Counselor Kimberly – Nature Walk*
5-6	*Dinner*
6-6:50	*Counselor Melinda – Music*
7-7:50	*Campfire Stories*
8-8:50	*Counselor Lenel & Counselor Melinda – Campfire Songs*
9	*Lights Out*
9-8am	*Sleep*

"Wait…this can…" I let my voice trail off as I realized I couldn't object to the paper with a negative word. But seriously, this couldn't be my new schedule! It had me going to see Teacher again! "Counselor Markus," I called out, "this has me going to the Art Barn… *again*."

"If that's what it says, then that's where you're to go," he called back without so much as turning around to talk to me. The jerk!

I was too stunned to say much else. What was I supposed to do? I couldn't go through another art lesson with him! Just my luck, it would be the same lesson, too! I mean, that made sense. If every group was going to each activity, then they probably did the same thing at each location, right?

"This is ridiculous!" I shouted at last. My mind went into overtime as I tried recalling if *ridiculous* was a forbidden word or not. It wasn't, I decided after a moment of panic.

"What was that?" Counselor Markus demanded. This time he did turn and face me.

My mind was suddenly buzzing with energy. I hadn't been keeping with the plan! The original plan that Wendy and I had come up with, the one for adding more words to their idiotic list! *Idiotic*, that wasn't on there either! My mind worked faster. If I was going to have to see Teacher for bad behavior, I needed to make it count.

"You heard me," I said without so much as a stutter. "I said this is ridiculous, idiotic even! The Art Barn is boring, dull, and dreary. I've already been there, so I know how tedious and drab the place is. Teacher is so slow! Brainless even! Having us do empty-headed tasks. This paper," I said while waving it in the air, "is *lame*, and I refuse to go back to that shoddy old barn!"

"Are you done?" Counselor Markus asked calmly as I paused for breath. His calm completely stole my thunder. My thoughts screeched to a halt.

"Uh…"

"Teacher, did you catch all of those?" Markus asked as he held his radio up to speak.

My eyes widened as I realized why he'd been so calm. He'd been holding down the button on his radio the whole time so that Teacher, and who knew how many other counselors, could hear everything I said! *When had they become so clever?* I wondered in dismay.

"Loud and clear. Send him over. I'll take care of the rest," came Teacher's cold reply.

I knew when I had been bested, but I wasn't going to give up either. I turned away as though I were leaving, which I also fully intended to do; however, before I had gone more than a step or two, I added one last thing.

"Well, this is just the worst!" I said loud enough for Counselor Markus to hear me. I chuckled to myself as I heard him start shouting the newest forbidden word into the radio. "Anyone else going to the Art Barn?" I called out as I ran out of the beach area. There was no response, but two others *did* join me. Together we ran away from the still fuming counselor. My pace quickened even more, but not because I was worried about Counselor Markus. No, I didn't want to be late to the Art Barn again. Teacher was going to be in a foul mood as it was, I had just insulted him after all. I just hoped *following the rules* was worth the consequences.

We were over halfway to the Art Barn before the youngest of the three of us stopped running. The other kid stopped with me, much to the first kid's obvious relief.

"Why…why are we…running?" the kid who had stopped first asked as he panted.

"I'm not sure if you heard me earlier," I began, feeling only slightly winded, "but I've been to the Art Barn before. Teacher does…uh, well. He is very strict, particularly with tardiness."

"And we're running to keep from being late," the second kid chimed in.

"Exactly."

"I'm Greg," he said, offering his hand.

"Hi, I'm Daniel," I said as we shook hands. It felt so oddly adult like, but I wasn't sure what else to do.

"I kn-"

"It's *understand*, now!" the first kid said, cutting Greg off before he could say something negative.

"Well, it's a…a…well, I…!" Greg sighed. "I give up."

"That's exactly what they *want* you to do," I said. "That's why Wendy and I are fighting back." I felt a twinge of guilt. I had wasted so much time on the beach talking to Tyler and then looking for a way to the canoes! I should have been talking with everyone, spreading the word and building up the resistance. Well, I could remedy some of that mistake right here and now.

"How?" Greg asked, eying me suspiciously.

"By following the rules," I said with a wicked grin.

"That doesnnnn…"

"That *does* make sense," I said. "We say what we want, but we are careful to keep from saying words that have been added to the boards outside of camp. You saw how Counselor Markus reacted? When I said *worst* and ran off?"

"Yeah."

"I bet if we push them enough or get enough words removed, the counselors will start falling apart!"

"Yeah!" both kids said together.

"But Teacher sounded…"

"Like he's prepared for you," Greg finished as the other kid stopped talking.

"Which is precisely why I was running," I said with a laugh at the irony.

"What? Oh! Because if we're late he can do something about that because you broke a rule!" Greg was the first to make the connection.

I was a little worried about the younger kid, but he seemed to understand why we were running now.

"We should hurry then," the younger kid whined.

Unsure of what to say to that, I shrugged and started us off again. We weren't the first ones to make it to the Art Barn, but we weren't late either. Not wanting Teacher to catch me short of breath, I slowed down to a walk a good distance away from the barn.

"What....what...are those?"

I looked to see where the kid was pointing. There were at least half a dozen tall objects standing in the grass off to the side of the barn. At first, I couldn't tell what they were, but the closer we came to them, the more distinguished their shapes became.

"He's removed them all," I said in astonishment. I couldn't believe it.

"Removed what?" Greg asked.

"The stools. He's removed all the stools!"

CHAPTER TWENTY-ONE

Gray Boxes

"Why would he remove the stools?" Greg asked quietly. He looked as concerned as I felt.

"Because they squeaked," I told him. "He wanted complete silence when we were drawing earlier. I bet he became so bothered by their squeaking that he removed them."

"Where will we sit?" the younger kid asked.

"I think we stand," I said quietly. It was mortifying to see all the stools outside, to see them all lined up in strict rows all along the wall of the barn, like they were lining up for a mass execution or something.

"He removed them because of the sound?" Greg asked, breaking up my dark thoughts.

"Yeah."

"What if he just removed them because he kn-understood you were coming?" the younger kid asked, his voice shaky.

I shrugged. I honestly wasn't sure if we would be able to tell how long they had been out there. No one had said anything during lunch about it, so maybe a later group had pushed him too far?

We were almost to the open double doors of the barn now. It was dark inside, as the only light came from the sun. Not really wanting to go in, but fearing the consequences of lingering outside, I stepped into the dark building.

The air felt colder inside, particularly when the sunlight faded from my back. I had forgotten how joyless the place had been. Even my thoughts felt sluggish with the depressing atmosphere, and I wasn't the only one who noticed it either. There were others already inside. They stood at their chosen spots, silent, still, and eerily vacant-eyed.

"Pick a spot, and be quick about it," Teacher commanded from the dark recesses of the barn.

Greg and the other kid disappeared from my side, as though worried what sort of punishment might befall them should Teacher associate them with me. They moved to the opposite end of the table and as far away from me as possible. Part of me, a very tiny part of me, felt angry at them for that, but the anger quickly died. In its place came panic as I realized that *I* still needed to pick a spot.

"For those of you still coming in, my name is Teacher. You are to pick a spot at either of the two long tables. There is a box on the table along with paper and pencils. You are to draw the box and the box alone, and you are to do so in silence. Is that understood?"

"Yes, Teacher," we said together.

We all woodenly selected our pencils and paper. If anyone made eye contact, I didn't know. I knew I avoided it. Something about the place just crushed the spirit. Of course, having to draw a gray square box as an art project rather than a bright bowl of fruit likely had something to do with it. Plus, gray? And a #2 Pencil? Where was the color? The life?

Outside with our stools, I realized glumly.

Teacher made several of us jump as a few kids arrived late. He gave them a "strike one" for their tardiness. Then, somehow, one of them made the mistake of talking.

"Talking is prohibited until your work is done," Teacher said coldly to the offending girl. "That is strike two. You would be wise to avoid any further strikes," he warned. He was in a dark corner of the barn as he spoke, but the wood burning tool in his hand glowed a fierce red on the tip, illuminating his face with a fiery glow.

Normally I would have been terrified, but the tool tickled a memory that I couldn't quite pin down. Everyone else went immediately back to drawing except for me. I stared at Teacher and his wood burning tool.

Not wanting to look like I was staring at him directly, my eyes settled on the boards that Teacher had been burning forbidden words into. I recognized one: *brainless*. I winced internally for that one since it was the one I had used for describing Teacher himself. It figured that was the one he had burned first.

He clearly hadn't had the time to do the rest of my list, but there were other boards on the table. I craned my neck a bit, pretending to be stretching, and read what I could. *Cretin* and *abhor* were on top, but *insa-* was hidden by another sign. *Insacure?* No, that had an *e* not an *a*. *Insane* maybe? The word size certainly fit the board. And *monot-* was likely *monotonous* or maybe *monotone*. Then there was *dreary* and *din-* which was possibly *dingy*? Lastly, there was perhaps my favorite one displayed in its full glory – *ludicrous*.

I found myself doing something I never thought I would do in that awful Art Barn – I smiled. The words totally sounded like something Wendy would use! In fact, it had to be Wendy's work. Who else was so bold as to take on the counselors?

I sighed then. If they were hers, then she was still following the plan, and here I was slacking off and drawing gray boxes.

"Do you really wish to push your luck?" Teacher asked.

Surprised by the sound, I looked right at him. Then his eyes were boring into mine.

I looked down, unable to respond.

"Or perhaps you would rather test the luck of those around you?"

My eyes snapped up. I hadn't thought he would go so far as to punish everyone else for my behavior! Besides, I'd only been looking at the signs. Or was he still mad about that whole *brainless* thing?

"I've already removed the stools from the barn thanks to you and Wendy. How much more would you have me take from them? Yet more words? Or perhaps you would like to remain here with me and let a different group of campers enjoy…what activity will your group be going to next? Ah, yes. The nature walk?"

There was silence then. Dead silence. No one spoke up, not to condemn me or to defend. Then I remembered, we were supposed to work in silence. Only the foolish or idiotic would have dared speak up or to have drawn attention to themselves. *Guess I fit that category,* I realized glumly. The silence though! It was unbearable!

"I thought as much," Teacher said, several seconds later. He was staring right at me as he spoke, which is why I caught what happened next. The corner of his mouth twitched up ever so slightly into a smirk.

I hated him so much! I wanted to punch him! No, I wanted to

burn all those precious signs of his! Burn them to the ground!

I looked away and took a calming breath. This wasn't the time or the place. He was baiting me, pushing me intentionally. I had to keep calm. His signs would burn, but not yet. I just had to stay calm...

Teacher watched and waited. It wasn't until I returned to my work that he went back to his.

An hour felt like an eternity in that place. My cube drawing was just a square filled in with several layers of graphite from my pencil. At some point I had given up on drawing anything realistic. It was such a mind-numbing exercise. The only thing that got me through it, and probably everyone else, were thoughts of the Nature Walk.

"Alright, children. Clean up your workstations. When you are done, you are free to go."

I looked up to see other dazed faces and even caught one kid as he stopped moving his pencil, its led long since gone. How he had managed to move the leadless tip over paper without damaging it and without causing any sounds, I decided I would never know. We all moved stiffly as we put our art tools back in the middle of the tables.

"Nature walk," someone said. The words spread slowly at first as everyone waited for Teacher to scold the offending person for speaking. When no such punishment came, more people repeated the words.

"Nature walk," was whispered all around.

"I hear they have rabbits," someone added.

"Rabbits," I said slowly.

"Rabbits!" "And lizards!" "Don't forget the fish!"

As one we all ditched our stupid papers and ran out the door screaming about differing animals we hoped to see. We had no time to waste here, we needed to make it to the Nature Center and start our outdoor adventure!

Once outdoors again, our morale skyrocketed. We were all talking at the same time, but no one cared. We were *free*!

CHAPTER TWENTY-TWO

Nature Walk with Kimberly

Finally! We had made it to the Nature Center! It was everything I had hoped it would be. Lizards and bugs and snakes in a variety of cages. The place even had a small pond with an impressive rock waterfall snuggled away in a corner at the back of the room. It had to be a coy fishpond! It had to be! I just knew it.

For once, we were all happy. There were no complaints as we each took a seat at the two tables in the center of the room. All the faces around me were full of idiotic happiness. Nearly all eyes were glued to the cages, looking for any sign of movement. Mine couldn't focus on any one thing long enough to make anything out. They kept darting about the room as I looked from the cages to the windows to the mysterious pond in the corner.

And smiles! We were *actually* smiling! How long had it been since any of us had felt joy? Legitimate joy at being at camp. And how could we not be joyful? There were lizards to look at! And snakes! And a bunny!

"Hello, Children. I'm Counselor Kimberly and –"

"Hello, Counselor Kimberly!" we interrupted, only all too happy to give her a proper greeting.

"– I'll be your guide for this nature walk."

There were several giggles as some couldn't contain their excitement. I had enough restraint to only smile at the news.

"To begin with, I would like each of you to reach inside the cubby of your desk and pull out the nature guide pamphlet within."

A few fights broke out as eager hands took the pamphlet of the kid next to them. The fights were brief, however, as no one really wanted more than one pamphlet. Luckily, the conflicts ended before there was bloodshed. And there would have been bloodshed, but only because it was unavoidable with all-out brawls. I'm sure I wasn't the only one contemplating flipping someone's chair over or exchanging blows, but only if I didn't get my pamphlet! Thankfully, I had no trouble in retrieving it as the girl next to me waited until *after* I had retrieved mine to claim her own.

Morale was high with our group, and grudges ended as we all held the precious paper. No one knew what would happen next, but one thing was certain, we were on the path to great things!

"Do you all have a pamphlet?" the amazing Counselor Kimberly asked.

"YES!" we answered in unison.

"Excellent! Let's skip to page four of the packet, the numbers are on the bottom right. Let me...help you...if you have difficulty finding it."

"Found it!" "I'm good!" "Got it!" Several more shouts followed as we all eagerly confirmed that we were on the right page.

"Excellent! Now then, let's begin with the section titled: *The Life Cycle of Grass*. Who would like to read the first paragraph for me?"

She was so amazing, we *all* wanted to read it! Unfortunately, she quickly selected some lucky kid in the front row. I hated him for that.

"My name's Brent!" the idiot said, instead of reading the paragraph like he had been asked to do by the ever-wonderful Kimberly.

"That's a lovely name," the incredibly patient and kind Kimberly said. It only made me hate Brent more. "Can you read the first paragraph for me, Brent?"

"Right! The life cycle of grass," he began, "is a process as complex as that of any other organism on our world. Like other plants, it begins from the smallest form. Can you guess it? That's right, it begins in the form of a seed. As the seed falls from the original plant, it is often carried by the wind, birds, or other creatures until it finds a suitable...spot of soil."

When Brent – who was surprisingly a good reader compared to most of the kids I had to listen to at school – paused mid-sentence, the words sank in. We were reading about grass growing.

"You're almost there," the suddenly-not-so-amazing Kimberly

encouraged him.

"From there…the seed will…begin its journey to…adulthood," Brent's voice died out as he finished the final sentence in the first paragraph. We all felt his pain. How could they do this to us? How could *Counselor Kimberly* do this to us?

"That was wonderful, Brent! Who would like to go next?"

"Are we seriously going to read about grass growing?" the girl next to me asked.

"Of course! How else would you be able to appreciate the nature walk unless you learn more about what it is you're seeing?"

"I think it would be more fun if we watched grass actually growing," I said morosely.

There were several groans of agreement. More were about to speak out when a shadow passed over us all. Counselor Kimberly jumped and she spun to face the large glass windows where something blurred by.

We all turned to look. The sun was at just the right angle to have shot someone or something's shadow into the room. I had thought it was simply a person, but no one should have been wandering around camp, so I wasn't sure. Besides that, our counselor's reaction had me on edge.

"Oh, this is ba…oh!"

"What was that?" I asked around the same time as several others in our group.

Counselor Kimberly had her radio in hand. She ignored us as she fumbled with the buttons. "I need assistance! This is Counselor Kimberly at the Nature Center. Craig, report in. Craig! Repeat, I need backup, *over*!" She clipped her radio back to her waist and ran for the entry doors.

We were all frozen to our chairs, horrified, and confused. Before I could work up the courage to move, the door opened. Kimberly tried closing it, to stop whatever was fighting to get in, but it slipped past her, or rather, *he* slipped past her.

"I'm coming lizards!" the boy shouted.

"Kevin! *Stop!*" Counselor Kimberly yelled, but it was too late. Kevin pumped his arm back and in an over-the-top swing and launched a rock at the largest glass cage. The glass cracked with the impact and the animal within went crazy. The large lizard swung its whip like tail at the glass, the force of it widening the crack. In a mad frenzy, it struck out again and again as though he sensed the frailty of the wall he fought against.

"Kevin, how could you?" Counselor Kimberly whined as she hugged the smiling boy to her.

"Uh, Counselor Kimberly, the grass–er–glass is cracking!" Brent called out. He was closest to the enraged creature, being on the end seat in the front row. All thoughts of envy toward him disappeared as I recognized his unenviable position.

"Wha–? Everyone get back! Iguanas can be very dangerous when upset. If he breaks free–"

"When," I said quietly, my eyes never leaving the ever-widening crack in the glass.

"–stay away from him. Their claws and their saliva contain salmonella. Everyone, get on your desks!" she shouted as she struggled to keep Kevin back. Out of the corner of my eye, I saw him wrestling to get free and run to the lizard.

The glass shook with the next impact. The crack splintered off into a kaleidoscope that encompassed the whole side wall, and then it shattered apart.

"NOW!" Counselor Kimberly ordered. We all scrambled up onto our desks.

We stood, wide-eyed and terrified, on top of our desks. The iguana, however, remained in the cage. His head tilted this way and that while his tail twitched, though it had ceased whipping it about.

"Let me go!" Kevin cried.

I risked a look in Kevin's direction. Counselor Kimberly certainly had her hands full. The kid meant business too! I was fairly certain I saw bite or scratch marks along with what looked like beads of blood on her arms.

"Who is that kid?" I asked quietly.

The girl in front of me somehow heard my question because she turned around and gave me a sad look. "That's, Kevin. He's…special. Or at least, he…has a condition. The counselors have been having a difficult time with him all day. He's supposed to have someone watching out for him. I think that's who Counselor Kimberly tried calling on the radio."

"I've heard his name mentioned several times over their radios, too" someone else chimed in. "Kevin's and that other one. Craig, I think. I guess Craig has been doing a … a…"

"Opposite of a good job," someone else supplied as the kid struggled to stay positive.

"Yeah, the first I heard of him was when we were being sorted into our groups," another kid added.

"I want the table closest to me to *slowly*, and I mean *slowly*, exit off the side furthest away from the iguana. Then I want you to go outside and stay there," Counselor Kimberly said as calmly as possible. Her arms were red and there was definitely blood on her from Kevin's unrelenting struggle. Despite that, I had to admire her for being so careful not to hurt the kid. Kevin clearly didn't know he was hurting her. He was too focused on the lizard, which was made all too clear a moment later.

"But I want the lizard!!!" Kevin wailed.

"Where is my back-up?" Counselor Kimberly moaned.

The lizard continued keeping his eye on us, but we each made it down without incident. As I passed by our nature guide, I couldn't make eye contact as I caught sight of the scratches and blood on her arms. It made me sad to leave her, but I didn't know how to help, and worse, I didn't want to try helping with Kevin only to get in the way. She needed an adult. Where was Craig?

Once I made it outside, I had a difficult time not worrying about the stressful scene inside the Nature Center. Then, out from the shadows of the building stepped two familiar and welcoming faces. As we made eye-contact, I hoped that Kevin's arrival had been an accident and not a way to strike back at the counselors.

CHAPTER TWENTY-THREE

Visitors

"Wendy!"

"Hey, Daniel! You'll —"

"Will you two keep it down," a girl demanded as she poked around a tree.

"Oh, hey. Uh…" I stared at Wendy's friend, unable to remember her name.

"Seriously, it's Kayla. Who did you expect to go wandering off from a group?" She continued keeping lookout from her spot behind the tree.

"Good point," I said, grateful to have someone keeping watch. "You're definitely not Abigail."

The two girls laughed at the truth of that. There was no way the shy girl would have dared do something this daring.

"Is Kevin alright?" Wendy asked, giving the side of the Nature Center a concerned look. We weren't near enough to see the doors or the other campers in my group.

"I'm more worried about Counselor Kimberly," I said, also eyeing the building with concern.

Kayla sighed. "We tried stopping him, but he shoved Wendy on the ground and bit Tyler."

I gave Wendy a look to see if she was alright, and when she smiled and shrugged, I did my best not to blush. Thinking about Tyler being bit helped clear my mind. The jerk probably deserved it.

"Camper," Kayla warned us a second before someone joined our group huddle.

"Who are these two?"

"I'm Wendy and this is Kayla."

"Wait! You're the one who had words added to the board outside of camp!"

"*We*," I said, indicating the two of us, "did that."

"Huh? Oh, sure. Whatever," he said dismissively. "That's so cool!" he added, turning back to Wendy.

"What's your name?" I asked, adding him to the same list as cool kid Tyler.

"Oh, I'm a nobody, but Wendy! Oh, man! You're famous, and it's only the first day."

"Thanks, Nobody. I would really like to talk to my friend now," Wendy said with the sweetest smile.

Nobody nodded like a fool and backed away. Then he turned and ran off to tell the other kids what was going on.

"We should hurry," Kayla warned. "We were supposed to be going to the restroom, remember. That alibi is caput if we get busted."

"Isn't the bathhouse a bit far from here?" I asked, concerned.

"It is, but we're doing stress relief, sorry, *yoga*, in the Dining Hall," Kayla grumbled. "We left when we saw Kevin running past the front office."

"Anyway, Daniel, I came here to see you," Wendy interrupted as she led us more into the underbrush where a small game trail led away from the building. Our trio were careful to avoid being seen through the windows. When we made it safely to the trail, Wendy began talking again. "We have a bit of a plan worked out, but I'm having difficulty in spreading the word. You seem to be jumping groups, which makes you perfect for delivering the message."

"You have a plan?" I asked stupidly.

"Is that a problem?"

"Well, it's just that Tyler and I came up with one."

"Tyler! That's *so* amazing. He's the best." Kayla sighed.

I shook my head but otherwise did my best to hide my disapproval of the guy.

"That's where Kayla and I got the idea too! Turns out, he knows these trails really well and lives close to here."

"Yeah, he said as much," I confirmed. Something about the conversation had me concerned, but I couldn't figure out why.

The sound of twigs snapping put us immediately on edge and I lost my train of thought. We ducked. Soon after, Greg popped into view near where Kayla had hidden behind a tree. I had forgotten all about him.

"Greg," I called just loud enough for him to hear. "We're down here."

"Hey, guys. Something's happening. You need to come see this."

"What is it? We're in the middle of an important meeting," Wendy said.

"Yeah, but Teacher and Mr. Petrel are on their way here."

"They're what?" Kayla asked, her eyes going wide.

"Shoot!" Wendy bit her lower lip and looked around. "How much time do we have?"

"I d-uh…"

"I get it," she said dismissively.

This was not the time for stumbling over negative words.

"Last I saw, Teacher was at the Art Barn. He could be anywhere by now though," I explained.

"Shoot! Alright, Daniel. What's the plan? Be quick."

"Uh, alright. Later tonight," I began, speaking quickly, "we were going to wear down the counselors in just our cabin. We'll work on freeing the others later, but we're starting with one." Wendy waved her hand to rush me, and I continued. "The younger kids will pretend homesickness, fear of the dark, and they'll distract and wear the counselors down with crying and yelling and all the things little kids do. Then, after a rough start to the night, they'll be too exhausted to stay awake and keep an eye on us. When that happens, we'll sneak out and meet up at whatever trail Tyler said to take." I vaguely remembered him being uncertain about the path, but I didn't want to add confusion to the already daring plan.

"Probably *Drimer's Path*," Kayla supplied. "That was the one Tyler pointed out to me earlier." At least *she* didn't look smug about remembering details like that, unlike someone else I knew…

"From there," I continued, "Tyler," I rolled my eyes as Kayla sighed, "will lead us to his house where we'll hide out until the camp is shut down for negligence."

"Sounds about right. Our cabin will join yours," Wendy said. "Let's go, Kayla."

"Right. Good luck, guys."

They went running down the barely discernible path, only barely visible among the trees and thorny bushes. It didn't take too long for them to disappear from sight as the path dipped down a hill.

"We really need to get back," Greg reminded me.

"Right! Let's go."

CHAPTER TWENTY-FOUR

No

With Wendy and Kayla on their way back to their group, Greg and I quietly snuck up behind our group. It didn't take us long to blend in. Not that Counselor Kimberly could have noticed. She still had her hands full with Kevin. From what I could see, everyone had made it out, and judging by the way Kevin was yanking on the Nature Center's door, the place had been locked up. The doors shook with his constant tugging, and Counselor Kimberly looked to be at her wit's end in trying to figure out how to stop him, no doubt a much more difficult task considering her inability to use negative words.

"Let me *iiiiiiin!*" Kevin screamed. "I need to free the lizards!"

"Oh, thank heavens!" Counselor Kimberly cried as she caught sight of something. We all looked to see what it was.

Teacher and Mr. Petrel were coming up the path to the Nature Center, but they were in a golf cart and moving faster than I liked. If they looked around as they drove, there was the potential they would spot Wendy and Kayla on their forest path...I pushed the thought from my mind. The counselors had no reason to look at wild overgrown paths...right?

Kevin screamed again, this time in jubilation. In unison, we all looked to see what had him so happy. He had the door open. *He had the door open!*

"He has the keys!" someone cried in alarm.

"Kevin, NO!" Counselor Kimberly cried as Kevin braced his hands on the side of the door, as though intending to fling himself inside the building.

Time seemed to stop as everyone heard the Counselor's use of a forbidden word. Even Kevin stopped moving. I couldn't see his face, from where I was, but I could see Kimberly's. The dread there was evident, almost as evident as the dark scornful looks of Teacher and Mr. Petrel.

"Kevin, no," Counselor Kimberly said more calmly, though whether she said it in defiance or simply because it had the desired effect on Kevin was unclear. She gently grabbed Kevin's hands and pushed the door closed. With the other, she turned the key he had left in the lock before finally removing it from the door.

"It is a sad day, indeed," Mr. Petrel said as he stepped out of the cart, "when one of our own fails to uphold one of our sacred tenants."

Counselor Kimberly closed her eyes but did not turn around to face Mr. Petrel. I couldn't blame her. I don't think any of us did.

"Kevin," Teacher called. "It's time for you to go home."

"Go home?" Kevin cried in excitement.

"Yes," Teacher said simply. "Would you like to ride back with me to your cabin? We can pack your things and wait for your parents at the front office."

"I'm going home?"

Teacher sighed, even his patience was being put to the test with Kevin. "Yes, Kevin. You are going home."

Kevin needed no further bribery. He ran for the back of the cart and jumped on. Teacher looked like he was about to let him sit in the back, but even he couldn't deny the danger of letting Kevin sit in a spot where he couldn't keep an eye on him.

"Kevin, sit in the front seat."

"I want the back seat!"

"Do you think you have *earned* the privilege of sitting back there?" Teacher asked coldly.

Surprisingly, Kevin gave in without another word of protest. I mean, Teacher was imposing and all, but Kevin had seemed so immune to everything. Still, it was probably for the best he sat somewhere that would keep him from running off to who knew where.

Without another word, Teacher put the cart in reverse before pulling away. Kevin's face lit up at the sound of the reversing golf cart, but his was the only happy face.

"Kimberly," Mr. Petrel began speaking, but only after Teacher had left.

She jumped at the sound of her name, but she turned to face him. Her cheeks were red, and I was fairly certain she was crying.

"You...hmm, those need treated," he said, pointing to her arms. "Report to the Nurse's Station. Emily is there now filling in for our absent nurse. When you are done there, you know where to go."

"Yes, sir," Counselor Kimberly said, sniffing. She began walking away slowly, but then Mr. Petrel called out again.

"Leave me your keys," he instructed. He held his hand out, palm up. She walked back slowly and deposited her keys in his open palm. Still sniffling, she turned away. Her arms came up across her chest and we all saw her shoulders shake.

It was so cruel! She was crying, and he was being so...so...callous about it! She hadn't done anything wrong! She had worked so hard to stop a crazy out of control kid from hurting himself and others, and quite possibly all the animals in the Nature Center. She'd taken hits from him, scratches, bites, and kicks. And when he had been about to do something else dangerous, she had stopped him with a word, a word she had every right to use!

Now she was being sent away, crying.

"This is wrong! She didn't do anything bad!" I cried out. I didn't care if I was using negative words! Someone had to say something! This wasn't fair!

"Daniel. This is your first and final warning from me for your use of forbidden words."

"Where was her first warning?" I demanded, ignoring his unspoken threat.

"Perhaps it is time you and I had a talk," Mr. Petrel said.

"Maybe it is," I shot back.

"Very well then. The Nature Walk is over. The rest of you are to head to the Dining Hall and prepare for dinner. If you are in need of entertainment, ask one of the staff for some help with the gameboard closet. I'll send word along that you have permission to use it."

No one moved, and I smiled smugly at the heartless leader of the camp.

He raised an eyebrow and someone shuffled forward. Then someone else moved, and then a few more. I looked around in disbelief as everyone began moving away. How could they?

"Cowards!" I called after them, but no one looked back. One by one they abandoned me and turned their back on the injustice of the camp. Then I was left alone with Mr. Petrel and his smug smile.

CHAPTER TWENTY-FIVE

Mr. Petrel's Office

It was a long walk back to the front office, and Mr. Petrel made it even longer by waiting for my group to walk further ahead. Apparently, he didn't want them too close in case we started talking. Not that I had any intention of talking. Besides, the longer we stalled, the better odds Wendy and Kayla had of making it back to the Dining Hall ahead of my new group. I hoped the unexpected arrival of more campers would make their absence less noticeable.

When we did finally start walking, I preoccupied myself with watching the group through the trees. We would be on the same path the whole way. The only difference in the route was that I'd be stopping at the office building while they'd be free to keep going. I saw them clearly a few times, but they were moving much faster than our ambling pace. Honestly, they probably never had any intention of hanging back and eavesdropping. No one in their right mind would have thought to do something like that...except maybe for either myself or Wendy.

Thinking about random topics helped pass the time, but it was still a boring walk. I did my best to avoid thinking about Counselor Kimberly's fate. Whatever it was, it wasn't good. I knew I would lose my cool if I thought about her because that inevitably led to me wondering what awaited *me*.

As my thoughts twisted in and out of the punishment that awaited the disgraced counselor, my own punishment, and all the attempted diversionary thoughts in-between, Mr. Petrel remained unchanged. He walked beside me in a stiff and somehow formal manner. I did my best to avoid looking in his direction. His presence was about as uncomfortable as Teacher's, if not more so since he was above Teacher in rank.

I kicked a pebble in my path and watched in satisfaction as it sped off down the path a good distance. *Where was the justice?* my mind continued to press. And why were so many kids at such a terrible camp? Were parents dumb enough to think this was fun for us?

No, they were selfish. They probably all heard of this super positive camp and thought sending their kid there would make them look good, and as a bonus, they got to have some free time. They probably didn't even care if the camp had a *positive* impact on their kid or not.

What a bunch of selfish jerks! I kicked another rock and sent it tumbling down the path.

"Are you quite done?" Mr. Petrel asked as another pebble skipped ahead. He stopped and frowned down at me, which only made my mood worse.

"How much farther is it?" I asked a bit sullenly. I could already see the flag post, which meant we were close, but I pretended not to notice.

"We're almost there."

At least with his office so close to the Dining Hall, I wouldn't have to walk too far for food later. When we stopped at the sidewalk in front of the Front Office, I couldn't help but look in the direction of the Dining Hall as I tried to see what the rest of my new group was up to. The angle was all wrong and the blinds were shut, but I could hear the faint sound of laughter coming from the building. I hated them. I hated them so much!

The cowards! They were only enjoying a good time because they hadn't stood up against Teacher and Mr. Petrel. They hadn't stood up for Counselor Kimberly whose only crime had been protecting a kid who *needed* protecting.

Where was the justice? Why were our parents doing this to us? I had a suspicion about why my parents had sent me to this camp. If they'd listened to my side of the story instead of believing the school bully, I wouldn't have been sent here. My parents had to of known this place would be a punishment for me. But I wasn't the one who needed a more *positive* outlook on life. *He* was.

Mr. Petrel took the lead and unlocked the office door. The lights were already on. Inside was the plainest office I'd ever been in. No photos, a desk with only a laptop, a lamp, a pen, and a pad of paper on it. In the two far corners loomed two large filing cabinets. As for chairs, there was a row of five uncomfortable ones near the door and a slightly less uncomfortable chair behind the desk.

There was a window next to the door we had come in from and a closed door on the other side of the room, no doubt leading to more dreary offices. The office wasn't just bare though, it was...*pristine*. Everything looked new, even the cushion free chairs.

"You may select a seat and join me at the desk," Mr. Petrel stated as he sat in the chair behind the desk.

I thought about leaving the chairs right where they were and forcing him to talk to me across the room, but somehow, I doubted he'd care. I grabbed a chair and slid it across the wood floor so I could sit closer.

"Pick it up," Mr. Petrel said through gritted teeth as the chair scraped the wood flooring. I hadn't intended to annoy him that way, but I was pleased, nonetheless.

Mr. Petrel sighed as I sat down. "Do you know why you are here? Why any of the campers are here?"

"Campers are here to obtain a more positive outlook on life," I said, spouting one of the camp's idiotic slogans. One which had no doubt been in the stupid camp video I'd been forced to watch.

"You're partially correct, yes." He tapped his fingers annoyingly on the desk for several long seconds. "There's more to it than that..." he paused, and his tapping fingers filled the silence once more. Then he sighed and continued, this time looking out the window rather than at me. "There are two types of children who are sent to us. The bullies," he said, his eyes turning away from the window to look at me, "and the bullied." He looked back out the window as he finished speaking. It was clear enough which category he felt I belonged to. Not that I cared. I'd already had my suspicions on why my parents had sent me to camp. Now that they were confirmed, that hardly changed anything.

"Does that change anything for you?"

I had to keep from snorting at the irony of that question.

Mr. Petrel's finger tapped as he waited for an answer. "Hmm, silence here usually means only one thing. Suppose I put it like this. Your behavior is that of a bully, and while you may see it differently, you should be more *sensitive*. This is supposed to be a safe place, a place for the bullied and the bullies to find a more positive out-look on life. How do you think my counselors feel when you bully them?" Tap, tap, tap... "What about your fellow campers when they see you trying to trick others into trouble?" Tap, tap, tap... "Do you think they feel safe?" Tap, tap, tap... "What do you think you are accomplishing with your behavior?" Tap, tap, tap...

I tried remembering what the last question had been, but all I could focus on was the annoying tapping of his fingers. And who was he to lecture me on people feeling safe? Had Counselor Kimberly felt safe? Had any of the campers felt safe when he and Teacher had shown up?

I kept my head down and my eyes on the floor, just like I had in the principal's office. Adults didn't listen to kids. I'd learned that then. It didn't matter if I had broken a rule to protect someone, they only ever cared about the rules. I'd learned that then, too.

"I see things are slow to sink in for you. Then let me put it to you this way. Continue down the path you have chosen, and you will remain with us for the rest of the week."

"What?!" My eyes shot up as I desperately sought some sign that the leader of this wretched camp was lying. He *had* to be lying! There was no way I could stay here a whole week. "Camp only lasts three days," I argued.

"How long camp lasts is up to the individual," Mr. Petrel's said evenly. "And before you argue any further, *all* parents are aware that camp could last longer for their child." Tap, tap, tap... "Good behavior is rewarded, Daniel. You would do well to remember that."

The door opened then, cutting through the tension. In walked a beaming Kevin, a cone of soft-serve ice cream in hand. He was followed closely by Teacher, who looked as diabolical as ever - stone faced, cold dead eyes, and his hands clasped behind his back.

But that ice cream cone...where'd Kevin get it? My stomach growled. All thoughts of bullies and punishment disappeared with the appearance of Kevin and his ice cream.

Mr. Petrel sighed and shook his head at the sudden interruption.

"I'm going home!" Kevin declared happily to me. He looked happy too. He had to be the luckiest kid in camp. Or was he the unluckiest?

Something else Mr. Petrel had said began to sink in. The camp was made up of two kinds of kids: the bullies and the bullied. What did that make Kevin? Did he have friends on the outside? Had this been his chance at finding a way to deal with the bullies in the outside world? A way to live a more positive life?

"Hmm, it seems something has sunk in after all."

My eyes darted from Kevin back to Mr. Petrel. He was watching me, his elbows on the desk and his chin in his hands.

"I believe Daniel has learned his lesson after all. Teacher, if you could escort him to the Dining Hall."

I stood woodenly. My head felt fuzzy and I felt like I'd been betrayed...somehow. The last thing I saw was Kevin happily eating his ice cream as he waited for his parents and the freedom of the outside world. I couldn't help but question what I was doing, what Wendy was doing, and more importantly, what the counselors were doing to us.

PART THREE

Evening

CHAPTER TWENTY-SIX

Dinner

Other kids were pouring into the Dining Hall, but I hardly noticed them. I barely even noticed the golf cart parked outside the office I had just left. What was I supposed to do now? I hadn't really thought of my actions as being…well, they were negative. But was I *really* bullying the counselors?

I certainly had messed Dave up, but he was abnormally cheerful… Was I making excuses for my actions? Did Dave deserve to have Wendy call him all those mean names? The only thing he had done to us was make us say our names in a positive way.

Then there was Counselor Melinda. Or had Emily met us next? Yeah, she'd been at the Nurse's Station. She had antagonized us for sure, and she certainly seemed to want campers to slip up. She might have deserved some poor behavior, but Counselor Melinda hadn't. She'd seemed rather nice, if a bit on edge with Wendy and I there. So had she deserved the *Know Know Knowledge* song?

Maybe Wendy and I *were* going about things all wrong. Maybe we weren't just hurting the counselors but the other campers as well. We were supposed to be a resistance, a resistance built on helping our fellow campers, not condemning them to a summer at this wretched camp.

"Hey, Daniel! How'd the talk with the one guy go?" It was clear Nobody was repeating himself. Had it been anyone else, I might have felt bad, but the guy was annoying. Was it wrong of me to feel that way about him?

"It went fine," I said, taking a seat at the table. As I looked around,

I noted the absence of Teacher. He should have been escorting me, but he was nowhere to be seen. He probably realized I didn't need escorting and had left me. For some reason, that annoyed me too.

"It went well," Nobody said then, breaking me out of my thoughts.

"What?" I tried to think back to what had been said and if I had accidentally zoned Nobody out again.

"It's *well*."

"What is?"

"You said that it went *fine*, but you should have said that it went *well*."

I stared at Nobody.

"Just ignore him," one of the girl's said from across the table. "He's been pestering all of us with his grammar rules. Or just plain pestering, really."

"Have n-!"

"Have too!" The girl quipped back before Nobody could recover from his near usage of a negative word.

He stood and forcibly wedged himself between two other camp-ers. They clearly were hoping to avoid sitting next to him. Not that I blamed them. The guy had been rather annoying.

"Sorry to hear things went…well, *fine* with the head counselor guy," the girl across from me continued.

"Yeah, me too." I had hoped that would be the end of it, but ap-parently everyone wanted to know what had happened. Normally, I would have been more than happy to share, but I felt too depressed. What was I supposed to tell them? To give up? That if they didn't give up and start being more positive that they would be forced to stay at camp for a whole week? What if by telling them I somehow condemned them?

"What happened to you?" "Yeah, what did he say?" "Please tell us!" "We—"

"Enough!" I said, cutting off their questions and demands. "I'm done."

"What does that—"

"If everyone could sit down and be *quiet*." Teacher spoke calmly, and despite the amount of ruckus in the large room, everyone qui-eted down. His presence was enough to quiet anyone, including the overly curious campers in my group.

"Thank you," Teacher began again. "The Nature Center is closed until further notice. Also, Nurse Pamela has recovered. She is now back at the Nurse's Station. All disruptive campers are to be sent there until further notice. That is all for this evening's Dinner Announcements. Camp Counselors, you may take your tables up for food. *In*," he raised his voice as several kids stood noisily, "an orderly fashion. If you would. Thank you."

"Teacher!"

It was Wendy who had called out the name, I was sure of it. What was she thinking?

Teacher stopped and turned. As Wendy stood, everyone else sat down. No one wanted Teacher's attention directed at them, and so they left Wendy to stand alone.

"What is it?" Teacher demanded coldly. His hands swung behind his back as he assumed his usual intimidating stance.

Honestly, what could Wendy possibly hope to accomplish?

"Well, since you ask. I noticed you said *disruptive*. Is this an acceptable word?" There were a few appreciative *oo*'s from the campers, but they were far fewer than usual, no doubt due to Teacher's intimidating presence.

"You are quite right." Teacher smiled smugly as the room turned silent once more. "As Wendy has pointed out, another word shall be added to the boards outside of camp. And to rephrase what I said before, rule *breakers* will be sent to Nurse Pam."

I rolled my eyes as Teacher changed the confusing nurse's title. Could no one be consistent on that? No one?

"Oh, well how odd," Wendy continued.

"Careful young lady."

"Oh, I am being careful. You can do the *opposite* of worry. Ah, speaking of opposite," Teacher's eyes narrowed as Wendy spoke, "you do seem out of sorts. I mean, this camp is all about positivity, right?"

"You would do well to sit down," Teacher warned, but to shockingly no avail.

"You see, you really are quite the *opposite* of what this camp is all about. You brood all day in a dark old barn, you take away positive experiences for campers, and you are downright...well, the opposite of positive. The opposite of Dave in fact. *He's always* positive."

"Wendy."

"Is it your name, perhaps?"

"Go see Psychiatrist Pamela." Teacher ordered.

I was stunned, to be sure, but not stunned enough to not notice yet another change in the nurse's name.

"You are just the opposite of good, or fun, or nice."

Teacher sighed. I could have sworn I heard several gasps. We were all on edge, just waiting for something to happen. This was unheard of! *What was Wendy doing?*

"It makes sense, with a name like yours."

Teacher's eyes narrowed dangerously.

Had Wendy discovered Teacher's real name?! Was this what she was risking everything for? She wanted us to know a man's name? How could she possibly think it was worth it? Even if his name turned out to be *Cruella de Vil*, what did it matter?

"Honestly, it was easy to figure out. There are two words on the boards outside of camp..."

"You have just cost your fellow campers dessert for the evening."

There were no groans of complaint, though I know I certainly wanted to. The sound just wouldn't come out.

"Two words that were added seemingly at random."

"And s'mores at the campfire tonight as well."

"It really is the opposite of a *wonderful* name," Wendy continued unabated.

"And all treats for tomorrow as well." This time there were groans, lots of them. "Do you wish to continue?" Teacher asked.

"Just the opposite." There was a stare down between the two, both daring the other to speak. Then Wendy moved. "However, I do believe that is all for now."

Wendy left. She just walked right out the door. Teacher followed close behind, no doubt to escort her, but still...

"Camp Counselors," Mr. Petrel stood and we all looked. "If you could begin taking your campers up. Radio me if anything comes up."

Then Mr. Petrel exited the same double doors Wendy and Teacher had taken. The hall remained silent for a little while, but kids gradually regained their voices. Even so, the noise level remained notably muted throughout the rest of dinner. No one talked to me after that. I wasn't sure why, but I was grateful for the solitude. I felt more confused than ever.

It wasn't until people began standing and counselors began ordering us around that I noticed dinner was over. Teacher's promise of no dessert had come true. I only noticed because there were several kids staring forlornly at the soft-serve machine. A cruel reminder of what we had lost, and worse yet, a cruel reminder of what Wendy's actions had cost us. As I walked outside, I couldn't help wondering if they were attempting the *divide and conquer* strategy. The thought faded as I numbly followed my group to our next lesson.

CHAPTER TWENTY-SEVEN

More Music Lessons

"Welcome, Campers!" Counselor Melinda called out as we made our way down the steps toward the benches and the stage. I was in such a daze that I had already forgotten that my next stop was back with the song counselor.

When I remembered that she had made us sing about our *knowledge* on the camp, my mind immediately went to devising another clever twist. Honestly, I wasn't sure how I could top my *Know Know Knowledge* song. I shook my head. I needed to start behaving myself, not making camp worse for everyone else. The less I did, the less they suffered.

"Ah, and welcome back, Daniel." Counselor Melinda looked a bit shaken to see me, but she recovered quickly. "Ahem, well, due to some rather creative methods, I have changed up our fun song time. Keep those smiles bright! We're still coming up with fun and wonderful songs! We're just focusing on numbers instead of words. So, pick a group and come up front for pencils and a clipboard with paper. Then write a song about a number...or *two!*" Counselor Melinda started laughing at her own terrible pun. Several campers groaned.

As I reached for a pencil and clipboard, Counselor Melinda pulled me aside. It wasn't far enough, however, as several curious campers leaned in to hear what she had to say to me.

"Daniel, I understand you are working on doing better here at camp, but I would like you to work alone. If anything happens..."

"I understand." And I did. I couldn't help but remember the shy girl who had partially paid for my *creativity* earlier. If I went down, that was fine, but no one else should have paid for my actions.

"Happy to hear it!" Counselor Melinda practically beamed at me. "Just so everyone understands," she said, raising her voice so everyone could hear her, "Daniel is going to be working by himself. Is that understood?"

Several campers agreed, which seemed to satisfy the counselor. I wandered off to go sit by myself. I needed to be alone anyway.

"Hey, uh…so I was hoping I could talk to you...for a bit?" some kid asked as he stepped in front of me. "I…I think you and Wendy are real creative." The kid kept his eyes glued to the ground.

"You heard her, I'm in a group by myself." I brushed past him and wandered over to a vacant bench.

"I kn-understand. I understand," he said, following after me. "It's just that I wanted to share something with you."

"Thanks…but I'll have to pass." There was an awkward silence as I waited for the kid to go away.

"It's…uh…my name…it's um…Terry."

"What did you want, Terry?" The words came out harsher than I had intended, but they had the desired effect, sort of. Terry did back away, but I could tell I had hurt his feelings. I hated that, but before I could think of what to say to make things better, he started talking again.

"It's just…well, we have that number thing to do…I'm…well…I think you are *way* more creative than me…that's all."

"Is that all you came to say?" Again the words came out harsher than I had intended, and once again I found myself cringing at my bad behavior. Terry didn't deserve my bitter words. I tried appearing apologetic, but Terry was looking at the ground again.

"I'm sorry. Did you have an idea for the assignment?" I tried sounding apologetic, but I just wasn't feeling much of anything.

"Well…have you ever studied another language?" Terry asked, only momentarily looking up.

"I've seen a few others, but I have…yet to study any of them," I answered, a bit confused by the question.

"Well…" Terry dragged the word out, wearing on my patience further with the delay. "Do you know the number nine…the number nine…it…it means something else in German."

I was about to interrupt, but the kid barely paused for breath as he rushed to explain himself, probably before I could stop him...or before he could be bullied. I brushed the thought away as I focused back on what the kid was saying. "...why my mom had me learn German."

"Why was that again? Sorry."

"Oh, it's fine. It's fine. The two brothers, they came over from Germany. It's my heritage, you see. She wanted me to learn the language they had learned, or something like that. And I've been learning it-"

"And?" I asked impatiently.

"And..." he looked around cautiously before continuing, "...the word N-E-I-N, it sounds like the number nine, but it means something else in German."

"What?"

"Oh! You kn-understand, it's forbidden."

I sighed.

"Oh...um...I kn-understand!"

I sighed again at his continued stumbling over avoiding the word *know*.

"It's the word Kimberly used when that kid went after the lizards."

Despite all my earlier desires to turn a new leaf, I couldn't help but feel a rush at the idea of getting a number put on the list of forbidden words.

"What's going on over there?" Counselor Melinda demanded, only now noticing us. Honestly, I was surprised she hadn't noticed *way* sooner.

"Oh, he was just telling me a really interesting story about how his -er- rather how two brothers had immigrated over here," I said quickly. My mind was racing as I went with the first thing that popped into my head. "It was a fascinating story about how they worked nine to five jobs."

That was it! I had my number's song! I was back.

"Oh...well. That sounds very...interesting. Um, carry on then," Counselor Melinda said uncertainly. The poor counselor had no idea what she had unwittingly sanctioned.

Terry looked paralyzed with terror, so I gently turned him back toward what I hoped was his original group. The movement must have helped because he took off without any further prompting.

In no time at all, I had my Nein song. It was a bit tragic when read the proper way, but it also felt somehow appropriate. I wasn't really sure what the two brothers had gone through as immigrants, but then I had heard living as an immigrant could be tough, so the song wasn't totally unreasonable. As I waited for my turn, I revised the final line, searching for a happier ending to the sad tale.

When the song was finished, I paused. I'd become so caught up in the moment, that I hadn't even considered what I had been doing. I'd written another song to bully an innocent counselor. What was wrong with me?

"Alright, Daniel. You're up!"

"What?" My head shot up. When had the other groups gone? I remembered hearing some of them, but I had been so focused on refining my work that I'd stopped paying attention to anything else.

There were a few chuckles at my expense. "All the other groups have gone," Counselor Melinda said patiently. She was so nice. She didn't deserve another awful song.

"I, uh. I have…" My mind went blank. How was I supposed to lie and say I wasn't finished when I clearly had it done?

"You can do it!" Counselor Melinda said, mistaking my sudden panic for stage fright. "Or…did you want help? I could have someone else read it?"

She had clearly forgotten her own rule of having only me to blame if something went wrong. I had to go. There was no choice now. There was no way I was letting someone else take the fall. Not this time. My face burned as I stood on the tiny stage.

Nein Song
Nein, nein, nein. 9 to 5 jobs.
Need bread and milk, so gotta work.
Nein, nein, nein. 9 to 5 jobs.
Got mouths to feed, a child on the way.
Nein, nein, nein. 9 to 5 jobs.
Have a landlord to pay, need to work.
Nein, nein, nein. 9 to 5 jobs.
Being an immigrant's tough. Just gotta find those 9 to 5 jobs.
Nein, nein, nein. 9 to 5 jobs.
Found me a job, now I'm workin' a 5 to 5 job. Mouths fed,
landlord paid, and a child on the way.

"That was wonderful!" Counselor Melinda said with a robust round of clapping. "And you made this up after hearing about Terry's immigrant past? Oh, how wonderful!"

I stepped down off the tiny stage, feeling a flurry of emotions. I couldn't look at anyone, but that didn't keep them from seeking me out.

"That was great!" someone whispered excitedly as I approached the benches. "Agreed!" "How tragic, but it had a happy ending." "How do you do it?" The congratulations and the questions kept coming, but I had to sit down.

"Reminds me of the railroad," a girl said, joining the huddle that had somehow formed around me.

"The what?" someone else demanded, Greg maybe? I wasn't sure I cared enough to find out.

"My mom told me a bit about it. So, I might not have things exactly right."

"But what does this have to do with a railroad?"

"I think she means the *underground* railroad," someone behind me answered for her.

"Exactly. It was a way for slaves to escape to the North. Anyway, they used songs to communicate things."

"Like hidden meanings?" I asked, suddenly feeling curious, despite my melancholy at having betrayed Counselor Melinda's trust...again.

"Exactly!"

"But what does this have to do with a railroad?" someone whined. He was immediately shushed.

The girl looked around to make sure that Counselor Melinda was still preoccupied. Satisfied, she began talking again. "The songs had hidden messages that the slave owners didn't...er...um, *think?* about. So, while they heard a catchy tune..."

"That was all they heard," I said with a halfhearted grin.

"Just like Counselor Melinda," Greg said.

We all turned to look at the counselor. She was still busy reading over my paper, appearing delusionally happy. Ironic, really...considering I'd sung her yet another *No* song.

"You were right..." I said slowly, still feeling sorry for the duped counselor.

"Oh, sorry! My name is Chelsea," she said, misinterpreting my pause.

"Well, you were right, Chelsea. Thanks!" I lied.

"You should be happy, Daniel," Chelsea said. "This camp is torture for us! Constantly fearing that...that we could slip and say a word that...that...oh!"

"She's right! You give us hope," Greg chimed in. It had to be Greg.

"They're taking our language away from us. Words that we need! You saw what happened to Counselor Kimberly. How was that fair?"

"Yeah, how was that fair?" I asked darkly. I still felt the snub of their betrayal.

"We're sorry." "Yeah, sorry." "Teacher scares me." "Me too." "And Mr. Petrel." "Yeah." They were all talking at once, offering their apologies. Honestly, how could I blame them for not standing up against Teacher and Mr. Petrel? The counselors had the power, not us. And they were abusing it.

"You guys are right," I said, ending their stream of apologies. "I'm...well, I might be able to use the railroad idea. For now, though, let's let Counselor Melinda enjoy the *Nein* song."

Our group dispersed then so Counselor Melinda wouldn't become suspicious, but she was still thoroughly enjoying my simple lyrics and mumbling something as the pencil flashed across the page. Was she erasing and respelling my *nein* to *nine*? Honestly, I really didn't know, or care. The resistance was back!

CHAPTER TWENTY-EIGHT

Journey to the Campfire

"Well, that was just wonderful!" Counselor Melinda said, calling us all to attention. "We have just enough time for the last group and then it'll be time for our extra amazing campfire stories down by the lake!"

That sounded exciting, but I couldn't help wondering if it would actually be amazing. Regardless, I kept my mouth shut. There was no need for me to ruin the counselor's good mood.

"Now then, Brian and Katina, you're up!"

"It's *Tina*," a girl, most likely Katina, said as she stood up.

"Oh…uh, right. Tina and Brian, you're up!"

I had to hand it to Counselor Melinda, she still somehow managed to sound just as cheerful the second time.

As Brian stood, I did a doubletake. It took me a second, but then I remembered him from the Toe Wars earlier. I'd somehow forgotten that he'd been banished from Wendy's group for my bad behavior. I couldn't help but feel some guilt for that. Of course, I'd also been the reason he'd been forced to *watch* Nurse Pamela's stupid video too. I was also the reason why he had to endure another round of Teacher and Counselor Melinda.

My guilt only increased as Brian and Tina made their way up the steps to stand in front of everyone. Neither of them looked terribly enthused. Brian held up his clipboard and looked at it…and looked at it. It was awful.

"Uh," Brian began slowly, "our *song* is about the number forty-two."

"Sort of," Tina said rather grumpily.

"Sooooo, here it goes," Brian continued, dragging his words out as though to stall long enough to avoid going. But it was no use. "Forty-two. Yeah," Brian sang…sort of.

"Forty-two, yeah," Tina huffed.

"It's a great number," Brian continued, his face going red.

"Yup, a wonderful number." Tina refused to make eye contact.

"A number that rhymes with two."

"Just as the ends of each line rhyme too," Tina said, finishing the painful song.

Had all the songs been this bad? I wondered guiltily.

"That was lovely!" Counselor Melinda said, sounding a little less cheerful than usual. "Well, that wraps up our song creation!

"Just for the record," Tina said, hands on her hips, "he wanted to talk about some silly book, but couldn-now actually had trou-ime…" She took a quick breath. "He had a time finding a word to rhyme with galaxy."

"I came up with smalaxy," Brian said softly.

"That's very clever, and I'm sure you could have come up with something if you'd had more time," Counselor Melinda said kindly.

"Proxy rhymes with galaxy!" someone shouted out.

"Alright, Campers! That's enough for now. We have a campfire to get to with stories and songs."

I stood and noticed a few others standing as well. The sun was getting lower, but I couldn't tell if it would be dark enough to even enjoy the fire. Maybe the counselors would take so long, it would be dark enough. I hoped so anyway.

Someone bumped me as I was making my way up the dirt and log stairs.

"Pssst," they hissed. "What happened to Kevin?"

"Yeah," someone else said, bumping into me from the other side. "You nev-ember…" The guy stopped talking as he fumbled whatever it was he had been trying to say.

"Kevin's fine," I said, somewhat surprised by the question.

"Yeah, but do you really think they'll send him home?" "Did they send him home?" "What if he's actually stuck here in some crazy place." "You mean some *crazier* place." "Did that girl really know Teacher's name?" "What's her name again?" "Anyone know where we're going?"

Everyone was talking at once and more people from the group crowded around. It was difficult to think clearly.

"I'm pretty sure Kevin's going home," I said quickly. "I saw his luggage on the golf cart as I passed by on my way to the Dining Hall," I rushed on. While I couldn't quite remember too much of that walk, I was fairly confident I had seen his luggage. Part of me wanted to share more about my time with Mr. Petrel and even how Kevin was doing, but I felt worn down. Too many more strikes and I'd be the one stuck here forever. Besides, as I looked around at the other kids in my group, I couldn't help but remember how they had turned their back on me and Counselor Kimberly. I wanted the camp shut down, but I wasn't sure I wanted to be all that friendly with people who had left me to face my punishment with Mr. Petrel.

"That's a relief!" "Her name was Wendy, you dolt!" "But what if–" The group's questions were interrupted as one of the guys shouted above the rest, "Seriously, where are we going?!"

Apparently, it was loud enough for Counselor Melinda to hear because she happily answered the question, though she was a good distance behind us. "You'll want to take the path to the right that leads past the big tree and goes to the Dining Hall. Follow the stairs down and to the left. Then you should see the benches, stage, and fire."

"That was oddly detailed," Tina said as she materialized beside me.

"Fire means s'mores!" someone else shouted behind me.

"They took away s'more privileges at dinner, remember Chelsea," her friend said rather snootily.

I remembered the pair from earlier, but I couldn't remember how exactly.

"Well it was someone else's fault, so go blame them and leave me out of it, *Macey!*" Chelsea sneered.

This wasn't going well, and I definitely had a feeling of déjà vu.

"Wendy was the one who did it," Tina said.

I shot her a dark look.

"What?" She looked surprised, and I tried letting it go. "I only said she did it, besides she–"

"It's more than you've done, more than any of you have done," I said bitterly.

Someone barreled into me, ending the conversation. I was about to push whoever it was back, but when I turned around, there was a girl crying on the ground. Standing over her, Chelsea and Macey were...slap hitting? Well, they *were* slapping at each other, but they also appeared to be trying to hit or push as well. Whatever it was, it was a disaster and was also the likely cause of the weeping girl being on the ground.

"Children, children! There will be s'mores some other night! The future will be better, you'll see!" Counselor Melinda said as she caught up to us and gently forced the two girls apart before helping the weeping one up. "Besides, it's such a lovely night for theater, and down by the beach too! Who wants to sing with me as we walk? Oh! We could sing *The Wheels on the Bus*!"

Several of us groaned in disapproval, myself included. Counselor Melinda broke out in song anyway, her voice and presence made it difficult for any further conversation. As I looked around, I saw that no one was making eye contact or even attempting to talk. This place, along with Counselor Melinda's song, was destroying us. We were fighting each other when we needed to be banning together.

What was this camp doing to us?

CHAPTER TWENTY-NINE

Missing

I heard groans from already seated campers as Counselor Melinda led us to two empty rows of benches. She was still singing the annoying wheels and bus song as she gestured for us to take a seat. Then she left us. The second her back was turned, my group started talking with the other campers around us, but I hardly noticed that. I was more interested in the area we were at.

We were seated at a section to the left of the stage. There were three sections total: a middle, a left, and a right. I wasn't sure if I envied the kids in the middle section or not. They had a better spot next to the bonfire, or rather a meager collection of unlit wood, and a better view of the stage. Although, having a better view of the stage didn't exactly feel all that enviable. If there was one thing I had learned from being at Positivity Camp, it was that *enviable* was not something that survived this place for long.

Counselor Melinda may have wandered off, but her song remained stuck in my head in a never-ending loop. I turned to the kid next to me, hoping he could distract me. That seemed like a safe thing to do, considering everyone else was already talking. It was Brian.

I was going to say something, but he looked...serious. At first, I thought he was having another Toe War, but his toes weren't moving, and his eyes were unfocused.

I turned to the person on my right instead, but she was already talking to several other girls, and about the girl's bathroom too. I'd only been to the bathroom twice, but that had been during lunch and dinner at the Dining Hall. I had yet to visit the bathhouse. Regardless, I certainly had no desire to talk about that experience. Girls were so weird.

"Hey," I said, turning back to Brian. I stared at him and he started at me. My brain slowly translated that we had spoken at the same time, but in the meantime, we continued staring at each other stupidly. "Go ahead," I said finally.

"Oh, uh. It's just that... Have you noticed?" he asked quietly. Apparently, it hadn't been quiet enough, however, because several heads turned in our direction.

"Noticed what?" I asked hesitantly.

"Wendy and that lizard kid," he began.

"Kevin," I said, nodding at him to continue.

"They're missing."

"Missing?" I said a bit too loudly.

"Who's missing?"

I looked over my shoulder to see the girl on the bench next to me, along with all of her friends, staring at us. Several other chatting groups took notice as well.

"Uh, well...missing from...from the fire. From this," Brian shrugged in defeat, the restricted language clearly hindering him.

"I think I understand. Well, it makes sense that Kevin is absent. He was sent home. As for Wendy..." I looked around worriedly, but it was difficult to see anyone from a seated position.

"That's what we've been talking about," the girl beside me hissed, bumping my arm to get my attention. She was one of the shoving girls from before. Her name started with a *ch* sound, I was sure of that, but not much else. "The girls have a network, you see," she continued, her voice barely audible. "Wendy was last seen-"

"Alright, Campers! Eyes front and center!" Some new and overzealous counselor called from atop the stage. "It's time to begin our story theatre!!" As he spoke, he danced across the stage before doing a quick twirl that ended with an extravagant bow. "Oh, do you hear that, campers?" he called out softly, his expression serious as he looked behind him, his hand cupped around his ear for emphasis. He was still crouched in his sweeping bow.

I looked too, but a moment later, I looked away, hating he had so easily tricked me into doing anything. There was nothing behind him but a lake!

"Oh! Looks like the camp across the lake is getting ready for a night of storytelling as well!"

"There's a camp across the lake?" My words seemed to echo as nearly everyone voiced the same question. Now I *was* looking. Sure enough, I saw a bright light across the lake, a bonfire maybe, and a darn good one too if I could see it from here.

"Hey!" the counselor atop the stage called out across the water. He waved his arms excitedly before turning to look at us. "Let's see if we can get their attention," he said, grinning broadly at us.

It took him calling out twice before anyone joined him, but in the end, he had us all shouting at the light across the lake. Just as he had us all unified, he waved at us to quiet down, and miraculously, we did. He stood up there, hand cupped around his ear as he leaned in the other camp's direction. I strained to hear whatever it was we were listening for, and I felt confident everyone else was too. Then I heard it, the far-off voices of campers shouting in unison, their voices coming from across the lake. I missed most of the first part, but then I heard it, "...got spirit, how 'bout you?"

I groaned, not because I knew what they were trying to say, but because of how undeniably lame the message had been. I should have known better.

"Did you hear that, campers?" The counselor asked as he sprang to a standing position. "They're challenging our Positivity Camp Spirit! Let's show them we're up for the challenge!" His arm pumped up into the air in his surreal excitement. "All you have to do is shout back: *We've got spirit, yes we do! We've got spirit, more than you!* Are you with me campers?"

There was a brief pause, and I had to give the guy credit for the way he was reading his audience. I knew I wasn't going to join in, and I found it likely others were breaking free of his spell too.

Then he was facing the water again, his hands cupped around his mouth. He gave a great show of breathing in, and then people were shouting the chant back. As near as I could tell, it was the older kids who dropped off first. The younger ones gave it their all the longest and the loudest, but in the end, the chant died down too much to have been heard clearly across the lake.

"That's alright, campers. We'll get 'em tomorrow!"

This time my groan was joined by several others. He'd *definitely* lost his hold on us. While I couldn't be sure, I could've sworn I heard laughter from across the lake, not much, but just enough. Real or imagine, it only made my hatred for our camp that much stronger.

CHAPTER THIRTY

Campfire Stories

"Alright, it's time to begin, campers! I'm Counselor Lenel from *House Cheer*! And joining me on the stage for tonight's performance is Counselor Dave from *House Jubilant* and Counselor Kimberly from *House Glee*!"

My jaw dropped as I heard Counselor Kimberly's name. I had thought for sure we would never see her again.

"But she's different," someone shouted, drawing my attention to the center group. Soon after, a few others shouted their confirmation as well. With all of us crowded together, it was difficult for me or the counselors to pinpoint who had spoken. It was great!

It wasn't until an unfamiliar woman joined Counselor Lenel on stage that the words sank in. I quickly found myself agreeing with the others. The counselor on the stage was *not* the same woman who had led our Nature Walk.

"Hold on campers!" Imposter Kimberly shouted, her hands raised defensively. "By now you've likely met Counselor Kimberly who leads the Nature Walk."

There were several groans of admission on that fact, and I saw rows of stupidly bobbing heads as others eagerly accepted the newcomer's words. I, for one, was not going to fall for whatever excuse the imposter gave.

"Well, my name is also Kimberly. I assist Counselor Pam at the Nurse's Station."

Well, she certainly sounded like all the other counselors as she too jumbled up the confusing nurse's title and name. But I still wasn't buying it!

"But I've been to the nurse's office!" a brave fool called out. "And you, you..." he stumbled to a stop, however, as he failed to work around a forbidden word.

"I work in one of the back rooms, sweetie," the imposter continued, unperturbed by the camper's concern.

"Brian," I whispered as I saw a flaw in her identity.

"What?" he whispered back.

"Ask her about her *House*!"

"Her *what*?"

"Her *House*!"

"Why would I ask her about her home?"

"Oh, for goodness sake. *I'll* do it!" the girl next to me - Chloe was it? - hissed at us. "What about your *House*? Which Kimberly was in charge of *House Glee*?" she asked boldly.

The imposter sighed before attempting to answer the question. "Kimberly H. oversaw *House Glee*. However!" she had to shout now to be heard over the ruckus that statement caused. "Since Kimberly H. went home early due to a family emergency, I am filling in for her," the Imposter Kimberly lied.

There were many cries of *awe* as campers fell for the *family emergency* bit. I, however, wasn't fooled. It was too convenient and too strange a camp for any of it to be true. No, they had definitely punished the real Kimberly for her use of a forbidden word. Then they had tried to replace her, thinking none of us would notice.

"But I saw her at the nurse's office before coming here!"

"And I saw a cop car parked outside the camp gates!"

"There was a police car?!"

Mayhem erupted as everyone began talking at once. Then Teacher appeared, seemingly from nowhere, and walked toward the stage. He stood there in front of the unlit pile of wood, quiet, ominous, and with his hands clasped behind his back. It didn't take long for him to be noticed. Bit by bit campers settled down until the camp became eerily quiet. Still, Teacher waited.

Behind him, the three counselors on stage bustled about with silent smiles as they made themselves ready for their performance. Counselor Dave had a green mop-like piece on his head and was grinning ear to ear as he waited.

Meanwhile, Imposter Kimberly had papers in her hand and had

moved center stage. Counselor Lenel held a red ball and knelt on the stage opposite of mop-headed Dave.

"Are we quite calm now?" Teacher asked us solemnly.

I tried to respond, but my voice squeaked betrayingly, so I nodded instead. I wasn't even aware of how anyone else responded. I was too busy being angry at myself for not being able to speak properly. He was just another adult in this lame camp, so why did he intimidate me so?

"While Counselor Kimberly respectfully answered your questions, many of you continued to ask more. Do you think that is respectful? She has been most patient with you, but I assure you, my own patience is wearing thin."

I gulped at the lack of tone in Teacher's voice. Luckily, my gulp hadn't been audible, despite the dead silence of the camp. Even the bugs were being quiet!

"As safety is one of our top concerns," Teacher continued after a moment of silence, "I shall explain the cop car. Kevin Cardel, as many of you are already aware, was sent home. His father is a police officer and was on active duty when he was called."

It was all just too convenient for me to believe! I mean, *two* Kimberlys? *And* a cop car that just *happened* to belong to Kevin's dad? I wasn't sure what else they could mean, but I didn't believe them! I wished Wendy were here to talk to and to see what she thought. Wendy!

"What about Wendy?" I shouted, my concern overriding my trepidation over confronting Teacher. Beside me Brian flinched. "Where is she?" I demanded, my voice somehow not faltering.

No one else moved. I wasn't even sure anyone breathed. How had Wendy done it? How had she stood up to Teacher before, and all alone?

Teacher turned his head in my direction. As our eyes met, his lips turned up in his usual smirk. "She is speaking with Mr. Petrel. Any more questions?" Teacher asked, his voice sickly sweet. He looked around, smirking at us, daring us to challenge him. "Good, then I believe it is time for the story."

Without missing a beat, Imposter Kimberly began speaking while Teacher made his exit. "Tonight's tale is that of Shel Silverstein's: The Giving Tree. The story begins with a young boy and his tree!"

I zoned out as best I could. My stomach churned as Imposter Kimberly told the story – a surprisingly only *slightly* butchered version, given the lack of negative words – while green-mop-headed Dave and over-the-top Lenel acted it out.

I'd heard the story before from my mother. Unlike her, I had found it sad as the boy took more and more from the tree until there was nothing left – like a parasite. The camp had found a winner of a story here.

My mind wandered in and out of the telling of the story. I was still tense from my confrontation with Teacher. No matter what I did, I couldn't focus on what I was going to do. At some point, I found myself watching the play, or whatever it was.

Counselor Dave, it turned out, was the perfect giving tree. Apple by apple, green mop strand by green mop strand, Dave ecstatically gave it all away. Leave it to him to look happy while losing his stick limbs.

Thankfully, he lost his green mop hair early on or I might've been focused on that the whole time. It wasn't until Imposter Kimberly said "The end" that I even realized the story was over.

"Up next," she announced, "Counselor Melinda, *the only one*," she joked, "will serenade us with song! Before she joins us though, we're going to light the campfire!"

hused grumbles and a few downright gleeful shouts, probably some pyros. The contrasting tones confused the counselors. They seemed to debate working up more cheer from the groaners with potential pyros in the group. In the end, they went with making the bulk of us miserable rather than worrying about exciting the pyros. While the call for more joy at the lighting of the fire resulted in the same lackluster response from most, the pyros more than made up for it.

So much for safety, I thought.

CHAPTER THIRTY-ONE

Campfire Songs with Melinda

Some counselor I didn't recognize did the lighting of the fire. He had the tiny sticks lit within seconds of using a lighter. While they went up in a quick burst of flame, it took several long and boring minutes for the rest of the meager pile of twigs to flare up. When the rest did catch, the result was pitiful. Even the once cheerful pyros in the group took offense at the tiny flames.

As the fire was lit, I used the distraction to look around, but there was still no sign of Wendy or Mr. Petrel. I hated to think what he was saying to her, weakening her resolve as he had weakened mine. As for Kevin, I knew I wouldn't see him again, not with Teacher having said his father had picked him up in a police car.

The fire spat and Counselor Melinda took to the stage. I debated booing but thought better of it. She hadn't done anything to deserve such a cruel response. Although, she did have a knack for putting terribly bad songs stuck on loop inside my head. Well, if she did it again, *then* I'd boo her.

"Hey, Campers! We finally have our campfire going and now it's time for some campfire songs. Are you ready?" Counselor Melinda sounded far more cheerful than usual.

For whatever reason, her question was met with enthusiasm from several sections. I tried reminding myself that she wasn't the enemy here. The camp rules were the enemy; those and Teacher.

"We're going to start with one of my favorite songs, *There's a Hole in the Bucket*. Once you catch on to the verse, feel free to sing along!"

In horror I listened to her song about a bucket with a hole in it. I listened to dear Henry's questions and dear Liza's attempts to help him fix the bucket so he could fetch water. Liza really ought to have given up on the guy long ago, but she kept helping. The worst part was the ending. It had started with dear Henry needing to fetch water but not being able to because of a hole in the bucket, and it ended with him needing water to help fix the hole in the bucket. It hurt. The logic hurt. What was this camp doing to us?

At the end of the song, Counselor Melinda laughed. "That sure was wonderful the way they tried so hard to fix the bucket. What do you think, campers? Was that a funny song?"

There were a few laughs, probably from broken souls, but then came the slow grumbles as campers recovered. The second those started, the next song began. This time the song was about campers marching one by one. It was a catchy tune, but I could tell it would get stuck in my head the same way the bus song had, and I hated her for that. For some reason, the tune also reminded me of a different song, but my head hurt too much to care.

"Well, that was the end of our twist on *The Ants go Marching*. Let's try a clapping song. I think several of you will be familiar with this one: *If You're Happy and You Know It*."

I groaned. Everyone groaned. It didn't matter though. The song began, and we had to endure the torture and the clapping as counselors participated. Worse yet, Counselor Melinda paused the song early on to say we only had one more song to listen to...unless of course participation stayed at the level it was at. Even I began clapping after that announcement. One more song? I could handle that...I hoped.

CHAPTER THIRTY-TWO

Final Song

"Well, Campers," Counselor Melinda began. "We are at the final song of the night. This song was written by one of your fellow campers. How exciting is that?!"

There were a few half-hearted cheers, but with the fire dying, the entertainment for the evening barely passing as entertainment, and the camp sucking the fun out of everything good in life, none of us were really all that enthused. While we weren't enthused, there were a few whispers as to whose song might have pleased Counselor Melinda. No one *wanted* it to be their song. After all, whoever's it was would be to blame for dragging things out.

"Ah, Mr. Petrel. What wonderful timing you have! I was just about to sing a song by one of our campers."

All eyes turned to Mr. Petrel as he sat in an empty section of benches. There was no sign of Wendy, but I couldn't be sure if she had already sat down before Counselor Melinda had spoken or not. If she was sitting, I couldn't see where. I was certain that if someone spotted her, whispers of her return would have spread through the camp.

"Please, continue," Mr. Petrel said. He gave those around him a stern look and all eyes turned forward again. No one could survive his intense stare for long. Even I had difficulty keeping my eyes on him. Luckily for me, though, he wasn't looking in my direction, so I stubbornly kept looking at him.

"As many of you are aware, many groups worked on creating number songs. This one is about the number nine and was written by camper Daniel."

The sound of my name had about as much of an impact on me as it did on Mr. Petrel. Thankfully, I had kept my eyes on him, so when Mr. Petrel took a drink from his coffee cup – an oddity considering we were at a campfire – I had the pleasure of watching him spit it out as Counselor Melinda announced who had written the song. I was even more pleased as Mr. Petrel began coughing, no doubt having swallowed wrong.

My face must have been beaming with pleasure as I watched the leader of the camp struggle to compose himself. I did my best to compose myself, but in the end, I had to put my head between my legs or risk being discovered. It was too good to be true!

"Shall I continue?" Counselor Melinda asked, ruining the moment.

I kept my head bent, hoping it would look like I was embarrassed to have my song sung. She just *had* to continue! It *had* to be my nein song she sang! Even with my head down, I could still catch the sound of Mr. Petrel coughing. I dared look up and caught sight of him doing his best to take small sips from his cup. His free hand waved at Counselor Melinda, but even I wasn't sure if he were telling her to stop or if he were letting her know he was alright.

Counselor Melinda cleared her throat, drawing everyone's attention back to her. We were all eager to see which decision she would make. She seemed about to speak, but then the unexpected happened. A chant began.

"Give us the nein song! Give us the nein song!"

I don't know who started it, but the chant quickly spread and rose in volume. I feared Counselor Melinda would realize she was being baited and she would side with Mr. Petrel, but then her face broke into a happy smile.

"Alright, alright! It's so wonderful to see you all so enthused. So, without further ado, here's Daniel's nine song!"

My eyes darted to see Mr. Petrel's reaction. His face had turned a cherry red and anger and indignation flashed in his eyes. He knew. He knew it was no *numbers* song I had written. Little good that knowledge did him. The camp had been so enthused, and he had been so incapacitated by his coughing that Counselor Melinda was doing the opposite of what he wanted. It was great!

As Counselor Melinda sang, I happily sang along.

"Nein, nein, nein. 9 to 5 jobs.
Need bread and milk, so gotta work.
Nein, nein, nein. 9 to 5 jobs.
Got mouths to feed, a child on the way.
Nein, nein, nein. 9 to 5 jobs.
Have a landlord to pay, need to work.
Nein, nein, nein. 9 to 5 jobs.
Being an immigrant's tough. Just gotta find those 9 to 5–"

"ENOUGH!" Mr. Petrel shouted over our enthused singing.

I glared at him. We were two lines away from finishing one of my greatest achievements at the camp!

"All of you! You are to follow your counselors off to your cabins *immediately*."

There was a flurry of movement as counselors struggled to obey his commands as swiftly as possible. One camper tripped over a bench, but other than a yip of pain, seemed to be alright. Campers were urged to quickly but respectfully stand and start moving in the direction of their respective cabins.

Meanwhile, up on stage, Counselor Melinda's face had gone deathly pale. Was she afraid she'd be replaced with an imposter, too?

CHAPTER THIRTY-THREE

Journey to House Joy

It was only when we all started walking to our cabins that I realized I had never actually told anyone about my plan to wear down Counselor Markus. I might have mentioned something to Wendy, and that was well and good for her cabin, but that didn't really help mine.

All hope of communication was lost, what with Mr. Petrel glaring at us all and all the counselors keeping dutiful attention to make sure we didn't act up. Unless…

I searched my pockets as casually as I could. *Yes!* I still had a piece of paper and my pencil. They weren't the best, but they would have to do. The sky hadn't fully darkened yet, but it was already too dark to see the paper properly in the current lighting, so I waited until we were closer to one of the lights over the main walkway. We were a few steps away from where we needed to be when I looked around.

It was only then that I realized how depressed everyone looked. "So much for *House Joy*," I muttered.

"Who said that?" Markus demanded.

I didn't mean to look at him, but then I hadn't expected to be heard either. Somehow, he didn't realize I had been the one to speak, and I wasn't about to correct him either.

"If you could refrain from speaking until we reach the cabin, campers. If you behave better tomorrow, I'm sure Mr. Petrel will bring back the s'mores and other fun activities. Until then, please behave."

Counselor Markus' words had the opposite effect. Instead of staying quiet, several campers groaned. Two of the more vocal ones I recognized as the troublemakers from before. I remembered Jackal's name, but I couldn't remember his friend's. I did, however, remember their talk about the younger kids being like babies. If anyone could cause a disturbance and make it difficult for Counselor Markus, it would be those two.

Before I could get close to them, Counselor Markus had us stop walking. After a few seconds of silence, he had us start walking again but then stopped abruptly when someone sneezed.

The pattern, brief as it was, reminded me of a teacher at school who used to wait until we were quiet to move. She would stop walking the second we started talking. Well, that might have worked on our way to lunch or recess, but we were heading back to a long boring night in a cabin.

If we could wear Counselor Markus down before even reaching the cabin, we had a better chance of him not waking up while we escaped. So, when he started us waking again, I coughed. As expected, we immediately stopped as he heard the sound.

A few more coughs, and he realized the ploy. So, when I coughed again and he kept going, I switched up my tactics.

"Uh," I said in place of a cough.

"Campers." Counselor Markus turned around to look at us with a stern expression. "If you continue to act like this, it will take us all night to reach the cabin."

"But it's dark out," one of the younger kids whined.

"And you didn– ... you did ... you..." The kid gave up trying to avoid a negative word and started crying instead.

"I told you they were too young."

"*Mitchel*," Counselor Markus warned the camper who had spoken up.

"Yup, too young, and you forgot to have them bring a flashlight to a campfire," Jackal said, siding with his friend.

Counselor Markus looked like he was about to lose what calm he had left. "Jackal, Mitchel, if you could set a good example for our younger campers, please," he said at last. "I suppose since staying quiet is out of the question, we should go ahead and embrace some good cheer."

His words startled everyone, including myself. How was I supposed to break him if he caved in so quickly?

"Now then, I believe you are all familiar with the song." Counselor Markus jumped right into singing one of the terrible songs from the campfire.

My jaw dropped. Mitchel said something under his breath. Someone stopped crying for a moment before starting up again much *much* louder. None of it mattered though. None of us could stop him as our counselor began singing and singing and singing all the way to the cabin.

I really disliked Counselor Markus after that. Not only did he stop us from acting out, but he made us all move faster. None of us wanted to prolong that awful song any longer than was necessary. The terrible tune distracted me from my original goal of writing a note, which I only remembered as we were all filing into House Joy's cramped cabin.

"Before any of you start climbing into your sleeping bags, I want you all to get your toiletries ready. Those would be your soaps, shampoos, toothbrushes, towels, loofahs, toothpastes, and a change of clothes, which should be your sleepwear. You'll also want a flashlight. Every night, the youngest campers in our group will go with me to the bathhouse and shower. Then I will come back and the rest of you will go in pairs. Is that clear?"

"Yes, Counselor Markus," we all said in disarray.

I hadn't really thought about showering. While the idea wasn't unpleasant, I was surprised we hadn't heard about it sooner. Then again, we might have heard it earlier and I hadn't listened... Either way, it did give us an opportunity to plan something without Counselor Markus in the way. Now *that* would have been nice to know sooner.

"Good, and if I hear any excess talking, I'll start singing again. Is that clear?"

"Yes, Counselor Markus!!"

What was wrong with these people?

CHAPTER THIRTY-FOUR

Finalizing the Escape

It felt like an hour had passed before Counselor Markus left with four younger kids to go to the bathhouse. I couldn't imagine how it had felt for the counselor. The second he had set us all loose to gather up our bathhouse bundles, A Million Questions Kid had started in on him. I hated that I remembered cool kid Tyler's stupid nickname for the kid, but it was appropriate.

"I think we have our distraction," Tyler said into the quiet.

I know I jumped at the sound. Since A Million Questions Kid had left, there had been an unspoken agreement from all of us to simply enjoy the silence. Tyler had broken that silent vow. As I turned to glare at him, he gave me one of his cool kid nods, which only made me dislike him more.

"What are you talking about?" Mitchel asked.

"I think he's talking about the plan for sneaking out of camp," Mitchel's friend and accomplice, Jackal replied.

"Yeah, Jiminy would make for a great distraction," Mitchel agreed.

"I know, right. And we don't even have to convince him to do anything," Tyler said with another nod.

"Hey…hey…you said one of the words," a familiar looking kid whined. I thought I recognized him and the kid above him as being the ones who had gone with me to the art barn. My suspicions were confirmed a second later as Greg's head popped up over the railing of the top bunk.

"It's alright Brennan," Greg said, jumping down from his cot.

"No one's here to correct us, at least for the moment."

"We could still get in trouble if they found out," Brennan argued.

"Anyone here going to tell?"

"Nope," I said, feeling more confident now that we were all finally able to talk freely without any counselors nearby to punish us. Everyone else added a negative word of their own as we all agreed not to tattle.

"So, what is this plan I've been hearing about?" Mitchel asked.

"We're sneaking out of camp and heading to Tyler's place for a bit," I said.

"Yeah, we're going to take the back trails to my place. I live just outside of camp. If we stay there for a bit, the camp'll be shut down for negligence or something like that. Then we'll all be sent home. It's that easy."

"And you're planning on having the baby wear down Counselor Markus with questions. Then he'll be too tired to wake up and hear us sneaking out?" Mitchel stated more than asked. "It's not a bad idea," he admitted.

"Anyone have snacks? We should pack them up and take them with us," Jackal suggested.

"Flashlights too, but we'll need those for the bathhouse first," I suggested. "We can practice dimming them with shirts or something, so we can see enough not to trip."

"But not enough to be seen. I like it!" Tyler added, again with a nod.

"Hey, we should have someone set a timer. I want to see how long they've really been gone," I added.

"I already have one going," Greg said. "I timed Jiminy earlier to see how long it would take for the counselor to blow up on him. Turns out he can handle about half an hour of questions without losing his cool."

"That's creepily impressive," I said with a shudder. I knew it had felt like forever for them to leave, but thirty minutes? "If A Million Questions Kid can talk for that long, he's got to break him by the time Counselor Markus gets back. If it's already past 9:30," I paused and looked at the alarm clock next to Counselor Markus' cot for confirmation. It was. "If that clock's right, we may be able to slip out in pairs and pretend like we're going to the bathhouse. But if it looks like he's going to stay up until we're all back, we'll take it slow and wait him out. I doubt he will though. It could be close to ten by the time he gets back."

"I told you I had a great plan," Tyler said, drawing everyone's attention.

I held back a retort thinking it better to keep from having any infighting. After a quick look around, I had the feeling no one else appreciated Tyler either. Or at least, Mitchel and Jackal didn't look too pleased.

"Sounds good to me. We'll play it by ear then," Mitchel said. He made a point not to look in Tyler's direction as he spoke.

"What's that mean?" Brennan asked in his usual tiny voice. It was clear Mitchel intimidated him. Actually, it was clear that just about anything intimidated the kid.

"I'll explain it," Greg said, pulling Brennan aside and whispering to him.

I turned away and started practicing dulling down my flashlight.

"Oh, one last thing," I said, turning around. "We're hoping to meet up with one of the girl's cabins as well. I'm not sure how well that'll work out, but that's the plan."

"Couldn't you just go back for them?" Mitchel suggested. "If we really have worn our counselor down with Jiminy or million questions guy or whatever he goes by, then we may have a head start on getting out. It could be a while if we tried waiting on them."

"Why not get us out and then slip back in with Tyler?" Greg added. "That way some of us still get out and we still have a chance of taking down the camp."

I found myself nodding. "I hate to leave Wendy behind, but you're right. We may have a head start on the girls, and I can always come back in and help them escape."

"I'll come back with you, of course, seeing as I know the way," Tyler said, once more adding little to the conversation.

"Then let's get packing," I said, doing my best not to roll my eyes as Tyler once again nodded at everyone in the one-room cabin.

CHAPTER THIRTY-FIVE

The Distraction

Counselor Markus was at his wits end by the time he and the other four campers arrived back in the cabin. He kept his flashlight on, but as he entered, he turned off the cabin lights. Directly behind him came Jiminy, the Million Questions Kid.

Somehow A Million Questions Kid still had questions to ask. The second he stepped through the cabin doors he asked if there were nearby restrooms (which there weren't. The closest one was in the bathhouse and required waking up the counselor or a buddy to go to). With that question answered, the kid switched to what to do in case of different emergency situations, health risks, spider bites, asthma, panic attacks, and bedwetting – just out of a general curiosity, he had said. The worst part about the questions was that they were relevant enough that Counselor Markus had no choice but to answer them.

"Enough, Jiminy," Counselor Markus said with a worn-out sigh. "It is well past lights out. Naython, Rett, and Zach. Please make your way to your bunks and turn your flashlights off. Then I'll want the first pair to head to the showers."

"Bu-" Jiminy began.

"Jiminy, if there are any issues, *real* issues, wake me up and ask me then."

Jiminy opened his mouth and Counselor Markus stared at him with dead eyes as he sat on his bed. "Is it really alright to wake you up?" Jiminy asked anyway. "And what *is* the best way to wake you? Do you ever punch people when they wake you up?"

Counselor Markus stared at Jiminy, his tired and blood-shot eyes unblinking. The only evidence that he had heard the questions at all was the way his eyebrow shot up at the question of punching people who woke him up. He seemed to ponder the consequences of punching a child in the face, no doubt considering if he could get away with calling it an *accidental reflex*.

I watched, eager to see how Counselor Markus would respond. It was clear by Jiminy's shifting feet that he eagerly awaited the answer, and more likely, that he eagerly awaited it so he could ask another question.

"Will the first two campers please go and shower," Counselor Markus repeated. He blinked and rubbed his eyes. Then he kicked off his shoes, clicked off his flashlight, and put a pillow over his face as he fell into his bed. He was clearly done with the world.

"But, what about my question?" Jiminy blurted out.

The newest question was met with a muffled groan and what could have been words as Counselor Markus responded from under his pillow. I wondered if he said any negative words. After all, no one would have been able to decipher what he said. Regardless, we had done it! We had broken Counselor Markus! Best yet, we hadn't even *tried* to do it. Jiminy had single-handedly taken him down. It was beautiful.

"Jackal, let's go," Mitchel said, taking the lead. As he clicked on his flashlight, he gave me a thumbs up and what I thought was a wink. It was difficult to tell in the shadows now that Counselor Markus' giant lantern light and the cabin lights were off.

Time ticked by slowly, but after what felt like five minutes, Greg and Brennan took their leave of the cabin. Once they were gone, it would be myself and Tyler next. I wasn't sure if the other four kids would come or not, since they hadn't been there during the plan, and it was too risky to try including them now. Besides, none of them flinched or said anything as Greg and Brennan left. I just hoped Tyler and I could slip out without notice as well.

My heart was racing by the time it felt safe enough to slip out. Counselor Markus had removed the pillow from over his face and had already started snoring lightly. There were a few swooshing sounds as the younger kids tossed and turned in their sleeping bags, but for the most part, everyone seemed to be passed out or were in the process of doing so.

Tyler was the first to stand up. He had the furthest to walk to the door, so I took my time in quietly slipping off the bottom bunk. For the first time, I was glad I hadn't arrived in time to claim a top bunk. A floorboard squeaked behind me as Tyler wandered over. I fought to keep from shushing him. The last thing we needed was more noise.

As quietly as I could, I positioned my flashlight inside my shirt and flipped it on. Counselor Markus stirred and I froze. Agonizing seconds passed before he went back to his light snoring.

Tyler nodded at me, and I grabbed my bag with my spare clothes and bathroom supplies. That way, if we were caught, it wouldn't look too suspicious. With one hand holding the flashlight and the other holding my pack, I didn't have a hand free for my shoes. I stuffed my feet in them as best I could and started for the door.

It was only when we were both outside and the cabin door had creaked painfully loud behind us that I was able to breathe again. That was when I looked up at the stupid sign that marked our cabin as *House Joy*.

That stupid sign had to go! I looked around and motioned for us to get off the porch. I didn't want Tyler to know what I was going to do, so I hung back a bit until I had a plan.

"Need to fix my shoes," I whispered at him just as he was about to say something to me.

"I'll meet you at the bathhouse," he whispered back. Tyler was gone before I could ask him what he had been about to say.

I shook my head as I turned off my flashlight and set my backpack down. Then I fixed my shoes and started back up the ramp. At least with Tyler gone, the group still had a chance to get away if I was caught.

Worried that overthinking would destroy my conviction, I easily climbed the handrail of the cabin, leaned over to the ledge that came about hallway up the doorframe, and then I was fully standing on the little ledge with my body smushed against the cabin wall. From what I could tell, I hadn't made a sound, yet. My mouth felt dry as I raised my arms slowly over my head and grabbed the plank that read *House Joy*. The sign didn't immediately fall away and I was forced to lift it higher and wriggle it loose.

The sign came away suddenly and I nearly lost my balance. I had both arms over my head as I continued holding the heavy wooden sign. I held my breath as I debated letting the sign go, where it would fall to the wood planks below and make far too much noise, or jumping down, which could have a similar effect.

"Go in reverse?" I whispered to myself, needing something to help me focus. I regretted not asking Tyler for help. Removing signs was really a two-person job. Then again, he would've stolen the credit anyway and given one of his ridiculous nods.

Thinking of Tyler gave me a burst of energy, and I used it to kick out behind me. My foot slipped or missed the railing entirely and I felt myself falling. Still stubbornly sticking to the plan, I kept from calling out. I hit the deck of the cabin with an audible thud. Worried someone would step outside to investigate, I scrambled to my feet, tucked the sign under one arm and ran. I only stopped long enough to pick up my backpack and flashlight.

Then I was gone, running alone in the dark as I made my way to the rendezvous at the bathhouse. As I ran by a particularly thick patch of overgrowth, I tossed the sign. I wondered how long it would take for them to discover it missing and the old cabin name restored.

"Wait!" I stopped in my tracks and looked back. I'd totally forgotten to read the cabin's original name!

CHAPTER THIRTY-SIX

The Rendezvous

I hesitated as I looked at the dark patch of overgrowth where I'd tossed House Joy's plaque and then back in the direction of my cabin. Did I go back to see the name? Or did I keep going? There was still a chance my fall had woken Counselor Markus. If I went back now and the counselor was looking for me…and if I were caught without a buddy…

With a sigh, I kept going. Some mysteries simply weren't worth the risk. Besides, *someone* would see it eventually and … and I would be hiding in some kid's basement. I gave another wistful look back down the dark path.

"Doesn't matter," I grumbled quietly. "Better to escape than go back for some stupid sign."

Still feeling grumpy over the loss of the cabin's true name, I walked to the outer reaches of the well-lit bathhouse. I hid off the path a few times as other campers returned to their cabins. Each time I thought about suggesting they come with us, but caution and fear over ruining the already questionable plan kept me in the mosquito filled shadows.

Scratching at more than a few red bumps from the thirsty insects, I quietly made my way around the perimeter of light surrounding the bathhouse. After a while, I thought I could make out the dark forms of my fellow cabin members around what I vaguely recalled being the start of a trail. As I approached, I saw the shadows shirk away and hesitated.

A flashlight flicked on, momentarily illuminating the group. Before it could switch off again, I made out a few familiar faces.

"Keep them off," someone whispered harshly at the light bearer. There were several more warnings followed by even more shushes to keep quiet.

"It's just me," I whispered back as the group quieted down again. "Is everyone here?"

"Almost," someone grumbled. It was too dark to tell anyone apart and I didn't recognize anyone's voice well enough to distinguish one person from another.

"We lost two of our people," cool kid Tyler explained. That voice, with its annoying air of superiority was easy enough to tell apart from the others. Even his shadow seemed to move as he gave his customary nod.

There was silence for several long seconds as I waited for an explanation. No one else seemed to notice, or care since they probably knew where the two had gone, and Tyler had always been exceptionally annoying at dragging things out. He probably thought it was cool to have long dramatic pauses.

Unable to take it any longer, I finally asked, "Where are they then?"

"Oh, they went to the bathroom," Tyler said with another shift of his shadowy form.

I glared at him, confident my expression couldn't be seen in the dark.

"I thought we left the babies behind. Couldn't they have just peed in the bushes? That's what I did."

I wasn't sure who had said that, but considering they mentioned babies, I figured it was either Jackal or Mitchel. Regardless of who it was, I needed to step in and prevent any rifts from forming. We would be stronger united. "At least they went together and followed the buddy rule," I said, trying to ease the tension. "How long ago did they leave?"

"A few minutes, maybe."

"Should be back soon."

I nodded. Then, as I realized no one could see properly, I said, "We wait."

"Yeah," Tyler said, drawing the word out. "We wait."

I took a deep quiet breath. We needed Tyler. He knew the escape route. He had a place to hide.

"What took you so long?" Tyler asked just as two dark figures came walking up.

"Sorry, it was crowded," someone answered.

"No, not you two," Tyler said, confusing everyone. "What took you so long, Daniel? I thought you only had to tie your shoes?"

I laughed, quietly of course. "I took down House Joy's sign. Now the real name of the cabin can be seen!"

I was shushed for my raised voice but didn't care.

"The cabins don't have real names," Tyler said, bursting my bubble.

"What?" My thoughts were echoed around me.

"Yeah, the original cabins didn't have names. It took Positivity Camp to give them ones. You took a big risk in bringing it down. We could've been busted!"

"Oh," I said, feeling my elation turn sour in my stomach. He was right, I could have gotten us all busted. I couldn't help but remember my fall and how loud it had been.

"Still seems worth it to me. Anything to strike back at this stupid place," someone else said. The sentiment was shared by a few others, but it was clear no one was too happy about the blunder. Luckily, they didn't know about my loud fall either.

"If we're all here," I began, trying to sound more confident than I felt, "then let's start. I vote we only have two flashlights in use. One will be for the person in front and one for the person in back. We'll want to shield them somehow," I paused. From the walk here I knew having no light in the forest could prove hazardous, but I also knew that having too much could give us away.

"Um…"

"What is it?" I asked, turning to look in the direction of the sound.

"Uh, well. It's just. On the way here, I used my towel. You put the flashlight inside it and point it down and then turn it on. It shields it better than a shirt, but I still saw sticks and things."

The kid went quiet and it seemed the shadows turned back to me. I smiled as I realized no one had looked to Tyler.

"That's a good plan. We'll want Tyler in front, and I'll be in back to make sure we aren't being followed."

"I could take the lead," someone suggested. "I found a stick when I went in the forest earlier. I can use it to clear the trail."

"You afraid of spiders?" someone snickered.

"Say that again, and the first spider I find is going down the back of your shirt." The dead sincerity of those words brought silence to the group.

"So, you'll go in front," I decided quickly, "and you'll clear our path while Tyler lights up the area ahead of you. Any questions?" I didn't wait for any questions. I'd seen teachers use similar tactics in school to force kids to move on. "Good, let's go."

"Can we...uh...put bug spray on first? I'm getting eaten alive," someone complained.

"Did anyone-?"

"I brought some. Let's just get this over with. Anyone who doesn't want it should move now. I'm spraying anyone who stays in range."

There was a click of a cap coming off and then someone began spraying. Thankfully, they were good about not spraying at anyone in the eyes, or there would have been screaming. How they aimed with such precision, for I felt the spray hit my neck, arms, legs, and front and back; I didn't know. Aside from the muffled bouts of coughing caused by the terrible poison that filled the air as bug spray was released, it went rather well.

"Tyler, go," I ordered between suppressed coughs. Not even Tyler objected as we began moving.

CHAPTER THIRTY-SEVEN

On the Run

We were quiet for the first few minutes as we all focused on the light ahead of us and putting our feet down without tripping all over ourselves. Then, as the excitement of our dangerous adventure kicked in, everyone began talking. Even I made the mistake of joining in.

Aside from Tyler, we all wanted to know where we were going, what to expect, what we would eat, where we would sleep, how long until we reached the house, and so on. We only had to shush ourselves a few times. Then the question about the girls and if they were going to join us came up.

"I don't think they will," I said. "There was no way to tell them when we moved out. The original plan was to wait until later in the night. Once you guys are out, I'll go back-"

A flashlight flicked on, illuminating the line of us. Then, just as quickly, it turned off. The air felt still as we stood frozen in our tracks. The only sound I heard was the beating of my heart. Slowly, Tyler, or whoever had the flashlight in the front of the group, lifted the shielded light up to where the other light had been.

"You guys are too loud."

It was Wendy!! I would know that voice anywhere! A second later the shielded light reached her scowling face.

"Wendy!" my voice creaked as my nerves got the best of me.

She shushed me.

"I'm glad to hear you were going to come back for us, but that's not necessary. We're all here now. Tyler, did you want to keep leading?"

"I'm the only one who can," he said smugly. Even from the back of the line I thought I could hear the girls sigh. What did they see in that guy anyway?

"From here on out, we need to stay silent unless absolutely necessary."

"Who put you in charge?" one of the guys in our group protested. "And shield your light next time!"

There were several shouts from both sides from those that agreed and those that disagreed. This was followed immediately by a round of shushing.

Wendy started saying something as we quieted down, but she abruptly stopped. She quickly shushed someone else, the tone of her shush silenced us all and put me on edge.

She spoke then, but it was too quiet for me to hear, and no one thought to pass the message along. So, I kept quiet and moved closer. All the while, I listened for anything abnormal.

Off in the distance, I heard what sounded like twigs breaking. The sound came from the direction of the trail's entrance. At least, I thought it was the same direction. It was so dark, and we had taken a few turns already. I bit my lip and kept quiet, terrified that Counselor Markus had followed after me and that I had doomed the whole escape over a dumb sign that hadn't covered anything.

"Coyote," someone said, loud enough for us all to hear. Someone else chuckled nervously, but then we all went quiet as we heard a bark. It was a muffled sort of bark, and suddenly, the idea of a coyote didn't seem so absurd. The hairs stood up on the back of my neck. We couldn't stay here. The sound had seemed distant but not nearly distant enough.

"Tyler, if there're coyotes, we need water. They'll lose our scent in water!" I spoke as loud as I dared and somehow my message was heard.

We began moving at once, our single-file line became a tight cluster as we all kept jostling to be in the center and not out on the perimeter. Everyone now held a shielded light. Despite my own fears of being discovered by a counselor, I couldn't deny the safety I felt in having light all around me.

We made good time down the hill, and my fear about our flashlights began to fade. No one spoke as we half-ran and half-tumbled down the hill. I even ignored the webs that clung to my hair and face.

After a short while, the path became more treacherous as we started hitting slick patches of mud. I fell twice on my own, but then someone pulled me down with them. A few quick fights broke out as others were pulled down, but for the most part, we kept quiet and kept moving. In no time, we were all covered in mud.

Our movement slowed considerably as we had to start going off path in search of solid dry ground. Only, there wasn't any. Several others lost their shoes as the mud thickened and deepened. Someone jumped over a log and landed chest deep in a pool of it.

The trapped camper called for help as he squirmed. Bugs, too light to sink, skittered across the mud pool's surface. A few used the log for support as they pulled on the trapped kid's arms, but it wasn't working. He was stuck. I'd have gone to help, but I had a problem of my own. My left leg had sunk knee deep as I had tried freeing my right foot. I couldn't move either.

"Tyler! You've led us to the mud trail!" One of the girls wailed. Kayla maybe? She would have been the one who had gone off exploring with Tyler earlier. If anyone knew the trails and where we were, it would be either her or Tyler.

"I know, but it'll slow the dingoes down too."

Dingoes? Dingoes were from Australia! In a moment of rage, I realized Tyler wasn't taking this seriously.

"Kayla, you take the lead," I hissed. "It doesn't matter how many of us make it out. It just matters that someone make it. Go!"

"No, you don't understand!"

An animal growled close by. Dingo or coyote, whatever it was, it was next to us!

The first growl stopped as another animal barked at the first. I didn't know if coyotes or dingoes barked, but it was clear they were working together. We were surrounded by a pack of the things. I pulled my flashlight out from under my shirt and swung it around. I was too scared to focus it properly and wound up waving it around uselessly. Someone else did a better job and pointed the light on a canine face.

Every light turned on it.

It snarled, and we all screamed. The animal howled its frustration. It clearly didn't like the mud, and its packmates didn't either.

Someone whistled. The sound was so shrill it cut through our terrified screams. The dingo-dogs yelped but retreated.

No, I realized, they weren't retreating.

"No," I said into the silence that followed the end of that shrill whistle.

"Yes," came the cold answer from the shadows. The dark form quickly became illuminated by every mud smeared flashlight our little band carried. I knew before the light hit him that it was Teacher we faced. The lighting only made him more eerie and terrifying. He loomed over us like a forest dwelling haunt that consumed the souls of lost and trapped children.

"How?" I said. We were caught. We couldn't even run if we wanted to, with our legs and our shoes stuck in the mud.

"Tyler, how *could* you?" Kayla wailed. The light shifted to Tyler as one by one we all looked at him. He didn't look concerned, he looked smug.

"You should've followed the rules," he said with a cool kid shrug. None of the girls smiled or sighed this time, and I doubted they ever would again.

PART FOUR

Night

CHAPTER THIRTY-EIGHT

Trapped

"You and I need to talk," a man growled as he stumbled through the underbrush toward Teacher. Several flashlights turned his way. With the added light, he stumbled less, but that did little to calm our shattered nerves. The light revealed his officer's uniform and his scowling face.

"I am aware of your concerns," Teacher said. "However, the children are unharmed by your K9s. Besides, at this point, they are all delinquents and therefore criminals."

"Our dogs...they're *children*..." the officer fumbled to find the words. He took a calming breath. "If I hadn't blown my whistle when I did," he began again, his tone menacing.

"Yet you did," Teacher informed him coldly. "And the children are safe. You are quite right though." Teacher turned to face the officer. "There are many things we need to discuss, including your son's early retirement from the camp."

The officer's face, which had been flush with anger a moment before, paled as Teacher spoke. I wondered if Teacher meant Kevin. If so, then the rumor about his father being a police officer had been true. It also meant his father led or was a part of a K9 unit. If Teacher or Mr. Petrel had known of our plans, which I remembered Tyler's smug expression when Kayla had practically called him out for betraying us, then we really hadn't stood a chance. What chance could we have had with trained dogs on our trail?

I turned my flashlight to Tyler, needing to see his reaction to all of this. He smiled that knowingly smug smile and gave that ridiculous nod of his head. Just who did he think he was?!

"Traitor," I spat.

He shrugged. "If you had followed the rules, you would still be safe in your cabins."

"Too true," Teacher said.

"But why?!" Kayla wailed. Several lights flickered to her, but quickly flickered away as it became clear she was crying. In fact, several of the girls were in tears. Even a few of the guys looked like they wanted to cry. This night hadn't gone the way any of us had planned.

"I've been here for *weeks*," Tyler began.

"That is enough, Tyler," Teacher said calmly.

"You made a deal to leave camp," Wendy said from the other side of the log.

"Yeah, I did. So what? I finally had a chance to leave, and all I had to do was find the bad apples in the bunch."

"Tyler, Tyler, Tyler," the words came out like a death sentence from Teacher. "You were to receive clemency for your previous behavior, but *only* for your previous behavior. With the uttering of that forbidden word, I'm afraid you'll be staying with us a while longer, and you'll be reporting to Counselor Pamela for your behavior."

"What?! No! We had a deal!"

"That's yet another strike. Do you wish to have a third and final strike?"

Apparently, that was the last straw because Tyler stopped talking and started fighting against the mud instead. He struggled but succeeded only in sinking further. Frustrated and defeated, he quickly broke down crying. While it was great that Tyler's scheme for himself had failed, it only made everyone else feel worse. If Tyler couldn't find a way out, how were we supposed to break free?

A different officer appeared shortly after that. She hesitated next to the pit of mud as though uncertain about what to do or where to start.

"Would you be so kind as to assist us in rounding up the children?" Teacher asked, the words coming out more as a command than a question. "You can start with the ones along the perimeter. The others appear quite stuck."

So began the lengthy process of freeing us all from the trap. More counselors arrived to help take campers away. One by one they took everyone except for myself, Wendy, and Tyler. They did, however, take our stashes of gear or at least the stuff we had managed to hold onto during our mad dash.

Tyler struggled at first, but with a look from Teacher, who had remained with us through it all, he settled down.

"Before sending him to Psychiatrist Pam, would you take Tyler to see Mr. Petrel? I believe the two of them have much to discuss."

"Of course, Teacher." The unknown counselor took Tyler's hand and led him away. They were escorted by an officer as well. Apparently, we three ranked high enough on the list of troublemakers to warrant such attention. I already saw two officers coming our way. They all had lights of their own now, or else they'd had them before and had avoided using them so they wouldn't give their location away.

I didn't care anymore. I just wanted to go home, and at that moment, I might've settled for a hot shower and passing out in one of the cabins.

Teacher fumbled with something before holding it up to his mouth. The action drew my attention as I worried about what nefarious device he had now.

"Counselor Emily," Teacher called over the radio.

My jaw dropped. I stared at him, suddenly very aware that *no one* had used a radio since we had been busted. That meant our entire capture had been expertly planned and executed. They'd even thought ahead to know that a single radio call could have given their location away. They were psychotic!

Teacher smiled as he noticed my obvious dismay. As he turned away as Emily radioed back that she was on her way. Wendy used his distraction to move closer.

"What is it?" she whispered to me.

"They knew the whole time. They knew our route. They knew to keep their radios off. They knew the whole plan. I bet our counselor was awake the whole time."

"Yeah. Ours passed out way too easy as well." Wendy pulled away before saying more. I don't know how she knew to retreat, but it was lucky she had because Teacher turned a second later. We'd have been busted for sure, though I wasn't entirely sure how a little whispering could make our predicament worse.

Teacher eyed us coldly. "I know you've both spoken with Mr.

Petrel before about your actions, but after tonight... For those who turn away from positivity, we have a special video," he informed us. "For ones such as yourselves. Well, it is clear you would do better learning to be positive in private than among others. For the moment, you will go with Counselor Emily and watch a different video. For your sake," he said slowly, "I hope its message reaches you."

"You sure act all high and mighty," Wendy taunted him.

"Wendy. Wendy. Wendy," Teacher said with a slow shake of his head with each word. He offered her a sad smile for her efforts.

"Yes, Creton Malefic?" Wendy asked in the sweetest voice I had yet heard her use.

The effect those three simple words had on Teacher were amazing! He crumpled! He visibly rocked back on his feet, his smile gone in an instant, and his solid pose of superiority vanished!

Then he laughed.

He regained his pose. No, I realized, he had never lost it, he had only *pretended* to lose it. "Ah, child. It has been a long time since anyone has broken into those old records. That may be my true name, but that hardly matters." He laughed again, a chilly mirthless laugh. "You will have to do much better if you wish to break me."

It was Wendy's turn to look uncertain. Where only a moment before she had been full of bold defiance, she now looked as scared as I felt. We'd been bested. Over and over again, we had been bested.

"You seem pretty confident about those videos," I said with as much confidence as I could muster. I wasn't so much worried about them as I was curious.

"Oh, you'll see what they contain soon enough," Counselor Emily said as she stomped through the mud toward us. She had tall boots on, like all the other counselors who had taken the campers away. They were so prepared! It wasn't fair.

"If you could free them so we might bring this night to a close. I'll be joining you for some of the walk, but I must speak with Mr. Petrel before anything else is to be done."

"I understand," Counselor Emily said, grinning at us. "Shall we begin?" she taunted, though the hand she offered for assistance seemed sincere enough.

CHAPTER THIRTY-NINE

New Video

It was a long and quiet walk to the Nurse's Station. The silence was made worse by the ever-present smirk on Counselor Emily's face. She really did have it in for the campers, I realized glumly as we walked. It seemed like ages before we saw the closed and barred gates to Positivity Camp and the Nurse's Station to the right of it. There were four police vehicles parked out front now.

To think we had come so far only to be thwarted. I kept my mouth shut though, like I should have done all day, like I should have done at school. They had been right to send me here, I realized glumly. Even if I deserved to be punished, Wendy didn't, and I felt even more guilty over dragging her down with me. *Why was I always getting my friends into trouble?* I wondered as we reached the steps to the Nurse's Station.

Counselor Emily opened the door and motioned for us to enter. Some other kid sat in one of the chairs in front of the TV as he watched the ridiculous camp video. He barely even looked at us as we came in. I didn't care, though. I didn't care about any of it anymore.

"You two, sit," Emily commanded as she intercepted Nurse Pamela.

"What is the meaning –"

"We should talk," Counselor Emily said, cutting Nurse Pamela off. "Outside."

The two of them left and Wendy and I sat down numbly in the chairs next to the kid. It was then that he finally took notice of us. He sat back and crossed his arms over his chest. Then he looked over at us slowly, his eyes glazed over with boredom.

"So, what do they have you in for?" he asked with a sigh.

"I'm Wendy," Wendy said by way of explanation. I followed her lead and spoke my name as well.

"*THE* Wendy and Daniel?!"

"Yup," I said morosely, "that would be us." I really didn't care for his ogling, especially with us in so much trouble. I also didn't like the way he was looking at her. Not that it mattered, I reminded myself. We wouldn't likely be seeing each other again after we watched some ultra-special video and were sent off to solitary confinement in the woods somewhere.

Before the kid could bombard us with questions, the door opened, and Counselor Emily walked in.

"Nate, you are free to go."

"Now? Alone?"

"Yes now, but what do you mean by alone? Did you come here by yourself?"

"Uh, well…" Nate was clearly struggling to answer the question appropriately – not an easy thing to do when avoiding saying *no* or else confessing to braking camp rules and traveling without a buddy.

"I came with him," a kid said, appearing at the entryway to Nurse Pamela's private office or else some other part of the Nurse's Station.

"Why were you…?"

"Nurse Pam said I could sit in her office and wait. She said I had been good, so I could sit and wait there, and-and…"

"Alright, whatever. Take Nate back with you to your cabin."

"Uh, yes ma'am. But…"

"What is it?" Counselor Emily asked harshly.

"Um, should I go that way or out the back?"

"What sort of question is that?!"

"Sorry, ma'am!"

"Exit out this way," Counselor Emily snapped, "and be quick about it!"

Nate's chair screeched as he scrambled to his feet and joined the other kid. Together they dashed out the door, only narrowly avoiding bumping into Nurse Pamela.

"Now then, Psychiatrist Pam, they're all yours," Counselor Emily said with a snide grin at us, one that clearly went unnoticed by her confusingly titled colleague.

The door slammed shut behind her and we were alone with *Psychiatrist Pam*. She slowly walked into the other room. I could hear keys jingling and then a file cabinet being unlocked and opened. There was a metal hiss as it slid open and then a clang as it reached the end of its track. There were some other sounds, but they were difficult to make out over the sound of the Positivity Camp video that was still playing, though it had at least reached the credits scene and only had a mildly annoying song playing as names floated up and away.

"Well, seeing as how you two refuse to be more positive, I think it's time for a parental intervention video," Psychiatrist Pam said as she re-entered the room with two small objects.

"A what?" Wendy and I said simultaneously. Under any other circumstance I might've found that adorable of us, but I was too stunned to do much more than shoot Wendy a quick look to see if she had noticed. I don't even know if she looked back. My mind was too jumbled to figure out much of anything anymore.

Before we knew it, a new video was playing on the TV and Psychiatrist Pam was moving away so we could see it.

"My parents!"

"Please refrain from talking while the video is playing." The command came out cold and heartless, but I clamped my mouth shut all the same, determined to not get Wendy into any further trouble.

"Hello Daniel, if you're seeing this, then that means your poor behavior is only getting worse," my mother scolded me, and right off the bat too!

"Positive language dear," my father said quietly as he patted her hand.

"How can I be positive about this?! They're having us film a video for *if* or *when* our son misbehaves!"

"Maybe you should let me do the talking."

My mother bit her lip. She looked so worried, and I felt so confused. What were they talking about? What was going on?

"Daniel," my father began, "your mother and I sent you to camp because of that incident at school. Do you remember it? You made a young man cry his eyes out because of your insensitive language."

"You called him fat! An obese dull-witted monster!" My mother's face flushed, and her eyes watered over.

"Maran, please, let me handle this," my father continued, using a calm tone, a tone he only used when he was angry, and I knew exactly who he was angry with.

"You were sent to camp so that you might attain a better attitude and learn to treat others with respect. I had hoped such a thing would be easy for you, but if you are seeing this..." He sighed heavily and collapsed his head in his hands. Several awkward seconds went by as he sat like that while my mother cried quietly in the chair beside him.

When he did finally look up, he had a hard look in his eyes, one I rarely ever saw, but always dreaded seeing. "Look, Champ, you'd best shape up. Since you are struggling to do so, it is our decision that you remain at camp for the rest of the week. It would be in your best interest to start improving your attitude. Shape up and be a positive role model for others, I know you can, Daniel." There was a pause as my father seemed to choke up a bit. "We love you."

My mother nodded furiously beside him and brushed the tears aside.

"We'll see you in a week, son."

CHAPTER FORTY

Unforgivable

The video was a few seconds too long as it didn't immediately shut off but instead had my parents sitting awkwardly side by side, my mother still silently crying despite doing her best to look optimistic.

"Well, Daniel. What do you have to say for yourself?" Nurse Pamela demanded.

I stayed silent, too stunned to respond and too much of a coward to say anything to Wendy.

"I thought as much."

"Well, if he won't speak up, then I will," Wendy said in outrage.

The tone of her voice shocked me into looking at her. She was furious, but her eyes were on nurse Pamela and not me.

"You're all a bunch of callous fools! Believing the words of some snot nosed brat as he whined about the names he was called and lied about them too! Did it ever occur to you louts that there was more to that story? That maybe Daniel was more hero than villain? I doubt it! It probably escaped your pea-sized brains that the teacher was also to blame! Allowing that bully to pick on a girl. That's right, you old hag! That nitwit picked on a girl because her period came unexpectedly, and she bled all over her seat in class. And that prick of a teacher refused to let her go to the restroom. Even when she said it was for her period, he refused! That-that-that ignoramus had kept her in class anyway. She stayed in the nurse's office the whole day after that, her mother too busy to come and take her home, with zero clothes to change into, and all the while that lying two-faced brat kept finding ways to pick on her! Well, Daniel stood up to him! Called him terrible names and asked him how *he* felt to be picked on for something out of *his* control! Maybe the next time you go looking for justice, you should *actually* look rather than believing the first kid that goes crying to mama. Fat shaming, ha! He even bragged about how he got Daniel in trouble because he knew what to say to get the adults going!"

Wendy sat back, her ferocious eyes locked on Nurse Pam's.

I had to speak up then, not for the nurse's sake, she was as white and as glossy as a wedding cake, but rather for my own pride.

"That's...close to the truth, Wendy, but I only asked him how it would feel if I called him short, since that was out of his control." I also wanted to ask how she knew any of that, but I couldn't figure out a way around saying *know*. Up until that moment I had been fairly confident that Wendy didn't go to my school.

"Wait, what?"

"Yeah," I answered, deciding I would ask her later how she knew about the incident. "He'd stormed off after that. It was only later that me and my friends, or rather the guys I had been with, heard he had gone crying to the principal."

"Seriously?"

"Yup, and when one of my friends defended me, he received detention for lying. And when that happened..."

"...then everyone else kept quiet," Wendy said, finishing the sentence for me.

"Yup."

"Th-that is! It-it's, unforgivable!" Pamela stuttered out at last.

"That's a forbidden word," I said dryly.

Wendy giggled.

Nurse Pamela's eyes widened fearfully, and I swear her eyes became darker as her pupils dilated. She had been white before with a red flush of anger tingeing her cheeks, but all color had since faded from her face.

"What is it?" I asked. Then it dawned on me, Counselor Kimberly had said a forbidden word too, and she had been replaced. Was the same thing going to happen to Nurse Pam? But would the counselors even believe us if we told them she'd said a forbidden word. It didn't seem likely, so why was she freaking out?

"I...I...I......" She crumpled to the floor, her eyes darting about the corners of the room.

"Holy..." Wendy muttered next to me, equally surprised, though she hadn't been there to see Counselor Kimberly (not Imposter Kimberly) when she had said a forbidden word.

"Chi-children pl-please. You-you have to..."

"Have to what?" I asked, now frighteningly concerned.

A voice suddenly came over a loudspeaker located somewhere in the office. The very idea of it being there both surprised and frightened me.

"Pamela Hilton, you are to report to Mr. Petrel's office *immediately*. Daniel and Wendy, remain where you are. A counselor will be with you shortly."

Before the final words were spoken, the door burst open. Counselor Emily ignored us entirely and went immediately for the crumpled form of Nurse Pamela. She hoisted the woman to her feet and was escorting her out of the building before the door even had time to swing closed.

"That's..."

"...abnormal," I said, finishing Wendy's sentence.

Our eyes met, and I saw my own fear mirrored in her eyes. Without a word I grabbed her hand and stood. We had to get out. My heart was pounding in my chest, probably loud enough for her to hear and probably anyone else who was listening in. I worried they could track us with the sound of it.

It was Wendy who ended up taking the lead as she took us further into the office. I desperately wanted to talk, to fill the silence, to say that we should look for a way out, that we needed to escape before the counselors could take *us* away, but fear of being overheard kept my mouth shut tight. Wendy was the one who found the back door.

We were outside in the warm summer night air again. It was nice to feel the breeze and hear the insects again. What was I thinking? Such stupid thoughts, we had to get out, not concentrate on silly insect sounds!

Ahead of us was the wooden wall that made up the entrance to camp. If we went left, we could be outside of camp with no trouble at all. Well, no trouble except for the sealed gate, the dogs, and the police officers, but we could easily have slipped under the fence! Or maybe climbed over it? Either way, we had to try! I tried pulling Wendy in that direction, but she wound up pulling me along after her...in the opposite direction.

"Where?" I whispered, my voice not sounding like my own.

"Keep up," Wendy whispered back. Then she let go of my hand and took off running. Fear of being left behind triggered a rush of adrenaline. In a cold flash, my whole body tingled and then surged with energy. I caught up to Wendy just as she slipped between two bushes. She paused a moment and then disappeared out of sight. I looked down and saw her below me on what must have been a trail. I followed her lead, slipped between the two bushes, and jumped down onto a lower trail next to the camp fence. It was a good four or five-foot drop, and my feet burned with the impact, but I didn't hesitate as I ran to catch up with Wendy.

CHAPTER FORTY-ONE

The Beach

By the time we heard the dogs, we'd already climbed over the stone wall that separated the beachy part of camp from the forest. Unfortunately, that had involved climbing down a rough cliff-like wall. Neither of us escaped scratch or bruise free, but we did make it down to the beach without broken bones.

Wendy was knee deep in water by the time I caught up to her. The cool lake water felt nice on my cuts. I did my best not to pant or look as winded as I felt, but it was little use. I was exhausted from the sprint down the hill and then the climb down.

"At least," Wendy began after she'd caught her breath, "those dogs won't be able to follow us."

I nodded in agreement. "Now," I panted, "what?"

We listened as silently as we could. The dogs had sounded too distant to be an immediate threat. Wendy drew my attention as she pointed at a dark mass on the other side of the small stream. Without waiting for me, she began wading through the water toward it. I quickly followed. While the wall and the trail may have delayed the dogs, it wouldn't keep them at bay forever.

Once we were on the other side of the tiny stream, the object we'd seen in the distance became clear. We'd made it to the stage where Counselor Melinda had sung my *Nein* song. Under other circumstances, I might've smiled at that, but I was too stressed.

Wendy wrung her shorts and I followed her example. The water might keep the dogs from tracking us, but that would do us little good if they followed a trail of water. The wringing didn't help too much, but it didn't hurt either. Luckily for us, it was a warm and humid summer night with a few strong breezes. With any luck, our clothes would soon be dry.

"We need to keep moving," I whispered.

"Right, but where do we go from here?" Wendy asked.

I pointed at the stage and started moving toward it when she suddenly stopped me.

"I think we should stay quiet around any of their structures," Wendy warned.

"Because it might be bugged," I said, realizing what she was getting at.

"Like the nurse's office," she agreed.

Concerned about being out in the open, I motioned for Wendy to follow me to the stage. Once there, we crouched behind it so we wouldn't easily be seen from the balcony area of the Dining Hall, which overlooked the area. We were both quiet as we worked on our own strategies on what to do next. Inspiration struck me first, and I motioned quietly for Wendy to follow me to the other side of the stage.

As I peered around the corner, I saw that the campfire on the other side had long since been snuffed out. I did my best to motion with my hands the route I had in mind. Then I made a swift move-ment with two of my fingers to indicate we needed to run. Wendy nodded that she understood, though I thought she looked doubtful of my plan. It was difficult to see her face clearly in the dark. It didn't matter. We had to keep moving.

With a deep breath, I ran along the water and followed it until I reached a fenced in area with a small shack at the far back. The beachfront looked different than it had when the sun had been out, and I was approaching it off trail, so I wasn't sure where the entrance was. It couldn't be helped.

Together, we hopped the fence and ran for cover behind the shack. A flash of light drew our attention back to the Dining Hall. Someone had reached the top of the stairs. The light became more ominous as the barking of the dogs filled the night air. I wasn't sure if they were on to our location yet or if they'd simply guessed where our trail would come out. It didn't matter. We had to keep running.

I pulled at Wendy's sleeve to get her moving again. It was clear she didn't know where we were, which made sense as I thought about it. I only knew of this place because of Camp Cleanup.

We took off down the beach toward where I had seen the canoes earlier that day. If we could free them, we'd be able to leave camp over the water where they'd have a harder time following us, or so I hoped.

We were winded by the time we neared the canoe racks. They were tall, maybe ten or twelve feet tall, and they looked alien in the moonlight. Without saying a word, we both clung to the edge of the cliff wall instead of approaching over the open sand. Behind us, the dogs continued barking, though we couldn't see the lights anymore.

CHAPTER FORTY-TWO

Canoes

"Pssst," someone hissed.

The sound came from the canoes and was so unexpected that I tripped over my feet in surprise. I fell down, hard. Thankfully, there was plenty of sand in the area, so the sound was muffled.

"Who's there?" Wendy called, her voice barely loud enough for me to hear, and I was standing beside her.

"We're over here," came an equally whispered response.

Wendy was the first to move. As she made it to the water, she quickly began tripping over her words. "How the? When did? What?"

At first, I was too alarmed to do much more than stare. In the water, not too terribly far out, was a canoe.

"Can you swim?" a familiar voice asked from the boat.

Judging by their size, the two in the canoe were definitely kids. Even so, I wasn't sure whose voice it was that I recognized. As I hesitated, Wendy started wading into the deeper water. Not wanting to be left behind, I shook my head and followed her.

"No, not toward us!" one of them hissed. "Go to the dock," he said and pointed. "The dock," he reiterated when neither of us moved to obey.

It took us a second to locate the darker form on the water. Wendy, who was still ahead of me, made it to the dock first. She climbed up and ran to the end of the pier and I followed after. The canoe took a little longer to reach us, but when it did, I saw who it was.

"A million questions kid?" I said, my jaw dropping. "How did you two…? When? *How*?" I found myself stuttering over my words, much like Wendy had done when she'd seen the boat, but I couldn't help myself.

"A mill what?" the kid, true to his nature, asked. "Who calls me that? Why would you call me that? Oh. I do ask a lot of questions, huh?"

"Shush," the kid next to him said. "If you're getting in, you'd best hurry. Markus said the dogs are trained and won't be misled for long."

Surprisingly, it didn't take us very long to slip into the boat. It rocked a lot as we climbed in. The older kid had been smart to have us enter at the end of a pier. Had we tried swimming to the canoe and climbing in, we'd have wasted time and would've likely tipped the thing.

"Thanks for the distraction, by the way," the kid said, all grins. "Me and me brudder needed a diversion to get to the boats. I didn't think we'd be leaving this early." Despite his obvious mirth, he kept his voice low and he kept his pace with the oars steady and sure. His *brudder*, as he called A Million Questions Kid, was attentive but mercifully quiet behind him.

"Wish you'd seen ol' Counselor Markus' face when you took down that sign! He was tryin' so hard not to rush out there. They knew," the kid nodded as he spoke, "they knew you'd be attempting to run. That's when me and me brudder knew we had our chance. We waited till the coast was clear'n we ran for the boats! I'd free'd the one earlier," the kid said, looking at me.

"You?" I asked. "Wait, it was you who wandered off during cleanup!"

Wendy shushed me as I spoke too loudly. Not wanting to be on Wendy's bad side, I kept quiet.

"Naython's the name. And that's Jiminy," Naython said, pointing behind him.

"Darn good sign," Jiminy said. "Did you see it?" He stopped with the one question as Naython turned his head to give him a look.

"I took it with me," I said sullenly. I remembered all too clearly Tyler's mockery of my attempt to take down the sign to reveal the cabin's former name. "There was nothing behind it."

"What?" Naython and Jiminy said with the same inflection and at the same moment that it sounded like one person had asked the question.

"Tyler said the cabins don't have any other names," I repeated.

"Not true," Naython said with a giant grin. If Naython hadn't had our attention before, he had it now!

"Do you know, Prometheus?" Jiminy asked, stealing his brother's thunder.

Naython sighed. "The name of our cabin was Prometheus," he filled us in.

"Sorry," Jiminy apologized. "Forgive me?"

"Aw," Wendy said.

She was looking at Jiminy and smiling. The kid was giving a sad look to his brother, but I didn't see what was so cute about that.

"Yeah, bro, I forgive ya," Naython said quietly. "Prometheus," he began, "was a Titan. A champion for mankind. He was known for his wit and cunning and he stole Zeus' fire and gave it to man. So cool. I bet all the cabins have Greek names!"

A dog barked somewhere off in the distance, ending our conversation.

"Sounds like they may have found the trail behind the stage," Wendy whispered.

"How do you know that?" Jiminy asked.

"I have a good sense of direction," Wendy whispered back. "It won't take them long to reach the beach, though the water will distract them...how much father?"

"We have family on this lake. Our mother doesn't know our dad sent us here, so we're heading to her house. Even if she'd known about the camp, she wouldn't have sent us," Naython whispered harshly.

"You know how we snuck out," I began, curious to know how they'd succeeded in evading Counselor Markus, particularly with him on such high alert, "but how did you get away?"

"Easy," Naython said with a wide grin as he looked at Jiminy. "Just one question. Me brudder asked to go to the restroom. Counselor Markus practically threw us out of the cabin!" Naython's voice rose to higher levels as he recalled the event with glee. "He was so darn glad to be rid of 'im that we made it here with no problem. Plus, you all caused such a ruckus that they'll not likely look for us two."

"Won't he miss me?" Jiminy asked.

I shot him a look as I thought I caught the slightest hint of false innocence in Jiminy's voice, like he knew what he'd been doing all along, but it was too dark to tell for sure.

The barking of the dogs turned into a hunting howl just as Jiminy asked, "What's *your* plan?"

Wendy was moving before Jiminy could finish his question. With a graceful motion, she was out of the boat with minimal splashing. I wasn't sure if I could follow her that well, but I did my best. As I went overboard, I was fairly confident my rocking of the boat didn't flip it, but I was sure that it came close.

Wendy was already treading water and talking to Naython by the time I resurfaced.

"...should be far enough. Thanks for the help, and good luck to you," Wendy whispered to the brothers before swimming for shore.

I uttered a quick thank you of my own before once again following Wendy's lead.

As we neared shore, I caught sight of a small stream and a rocky outcropping that may have been a natural waterfall. Wendy had apparently seen it too, because she was already heading for it. If we could climb the rocky wall, the dogs would be thwarted once again in their search for us. That, and if we stayed in the water, they'd lose our trail altogether. What luck!

"Looks like we got lucky finding them," Wendy whispered as we trudged our way through the stream toward the very mild waterfall. Neither of us bothered ringing our clothes free of the water. There was no time. It sounded as though the dogs had already made it to the shack. Even with the boat ride, we didn't have much time to find cover.

"Agreed," I said, after I realized she couldn't see me nodding.

"The counselors will likely see the canoe missing," Wendy continued. "If they see those two on the water, they'll see two kids and probably assume it's us."

"And if they don't see them?" I asked.

"They'll probably still see the canoe missing and think we left camp. That *means* they won't be looking for us inside the camp walls." Wendy giggled quietly.

I felt my spirits lift at the idea. "And the dogs will lose our scent with the water. We could do anything," I whispered excitedly. "While they look for us outside the walls, we'll be bringing the camp down from the inside."

CHAPTER FORTY-THREE

Rumors

It was slow going as we made it up the waterfall. We both slipped more than once, and I winced as I felt a thorn prick the palm of my hand. All the while, we could hear the K9s coming closer. By the time we reached the top of the meager waterfall, we were both a bit winded.

"You hear that?" Wendy asked, her breath coming in fast.

"What?" I asked, panicking.

"The dogs, they've lost our trail."

I listened and heard the sound of whining. The animals must have picked up our trail at the docks only to lose them again when we jumped in the water. I smiled.

"Where do you think we are?" Wendy asked, looking around at the dark forest. Her feet were still in the water, same as mine. We were both standing in a tiny creek with slow moving water.

I did a little calculating in my head as I tried picturing the camp's layout. I smiled wickedly as I realized where we were and what mischief we could cause.

"We're somewhere near the boy's cabins, I think."

"Then we're practically back where we started," she whined. I felt bad for her then and let her in on my plan.

"You heard Jiminy and Naython. The counselors are all over the place right now. I bet we could remove the signs over the cabins," I finished.

Wendy's face brightened at the idea. "We should take cover," she whispered suddenly.

I moved reflexively after her just as I caught sight of the glimmer

of flashlights back in the direction of the canoes. They were searching the water and the cliff wall. If we stayed put, we'd be found.

As confident as I was about not being caught, my confidence
faded as we had to leave the creek and start making our way through
the underbrush. There were fewer flashes of light as the counselors
lost our trail, but that didn't help quiet my fears.

I stopped walking and hid behind a tall tree and waited for
Wendy to catch up. We were nearly to the cabins now. A few twigs
snapped as Wendy found me. I cringed at the sound. I hated to think
what would happen if the counselors were waiting nearby, their
flashlights off as they waited in ambush.

There was little we could do to avoid unseen things on the
ground, not without any flashlights of our own. Besides, I told myself, they would have given us away in any case.

"Sorry, can't see," Wendy whispered as she came closer. "I've
been thinking. Do you remember how the speakers came on immediately after Nurse Pam said a forbidden word? Well, I'd heard
rumors that one girl who's been here for a month swears are true.
She and the rumor say the place is rigged."

"Wait, a month? That's not possible," I argued, my voice rising
unintentionally.

"Shush. Yes. Tyler isn't the only one who's been trapped here.
They reset the signs for the next batch of campers. Resetting them
is also supposed to help reset the negative camper's record. They're
then given a chance to change and be more positive, but one slip
up and they're stuck again whereas everyone else can make a few
mistakes. But you're missing the point!"

Wendy stopped talking and took a deep breath. I didn't blame
her. This camp had my own nerves fried, and that was before I'd
heard of the place being bugged. Even so, I wasn't about to abandon
my plan to bring down the camp. If anything, I was confident taking
it down was the right decision. They were tormenting kids and probably feeding their parents' lies just to keep them here.

"The point is, they have microphones and speakers in different
places, and I don't know where they are, how many there are, or
even how diligently they're listened to."

"And Nurse Pam was heard pretty immediately," I whispered
back. "It doesn't matter," I said after a short pause. "I have a plan
to bring the camp down. They might be able to fool our parents,

but those cops still care about our safety. I bet if we can prove the place is as corrupt as Kevin's dad believes, and prove it to the other officers, they'll be forced to do something even if Teacher has something over them."

"I'd wondered if that was Kevin's dad," Wendy said, her white smile visible in the dark. "What's the plan?"

"I'd rather not say it out loud," I said after a moment's thought.

"Right. Let's do what we came here to do and then move on to the next thing."

"Wait, how will I know you're still following? If we stay quiet, we could lose each other."

Wendy smiled again. Then she began fussing with some part of her clothing. I looked on in confusion. Before I could ask what she was doing, she handed me something.

"We'll both hold onto this. I thought it might come in handy, I just didn't think I'd have to use it for this."

"What is it?"

"Ha, it's a funny story actually. My mom gave it to me in case of an emergency. It's a wristband that turns into a long rope. It's really meant for if you go hiking in the mountains, but she gets overly worried."

"And Teacher didn't think to take it when he took all our supplies because it looked like a fashion accessory," I said in awe of her cunning. I was glad Wendy was on our side.

"We'll do three tugs for stop," Wendy started to explain. She stopped talking as a flash of light flickered far off. Then it was gone. Even so, it was enough to make us both nervous.

I hated not knowing where the counselors were, but we had a mission to complete. The longer we waited, the less we accomplished.

"I can't wait for this night to be over," Wendy sighed as the light didn't come back. "Let's wait to tie the rope until after we finish up here," she suggested. "I'd rather not wait any longer. If we're caught, we're caught."

"But if *not*," I said, letting the mischievous thought hang in the air.

Wendy giggled, and we moved out.

CHAPTER FORTY-FOUR

True Names

We stopped just shy of reaching the back of the cabins as a new light flooded the area. All the cabins were opening their doors. I clearly heard the mumbles and complaints as sleepy kids were ushered outside. The counselors looked just as upset as the campers as they worked to get everyone moving. They weren't, however, so out of it as to not threaten campers who spoke forbidden words.

It was only when all the cabins had been emptied that either of us felt safe enough to speak, and even then, our voices were hushed.

"Where are they going?" I asked first.

"Probably the main hall," Wendy said. "They must want to count all the campers and keep an eye on them. Maybe they noticed Jiminy and Naython escaped. It'll be easier to communicate and count heads with everyone in one spot."

"Then this *is* the perfect time to take down the signs," I said excitedly.

Wendy giggled.

Together we rushed up to the first cabin. Since I had already removed one sign from my own cabin, I took the lead by climbing up on the railing of the nearest cabin. Once more, I leaned against the wall for support before lifting the false sign free. Then I handed it to Wendy who ran off with it.

I wasn't entirely sure where she went with the first sign, or the second, or any of the rest of them. She was always back by the time I was ready to hand her one of the wooden boards. We had the signs for the boy's cabins all removed in no time.

As we worked, I happily took note of the names beneath the camp's signs. I released Oceanus, Cronus, Hyperion, and more. Each unveiling left me smiling as I pretended that I was liberating the titans.

When we were done with the names for the boy's cabins, I followed after Wendy as she ran for the edge of trees. However, she stopped at a suspicious pile of wood near the edge of the woods. We were far enough away from the cabins that I felt safe talking in whispers again.

"Those the fake names?" I asked, confident I already knew the answer.

"Yup," she whispered back. "I'll take half and you take the other half."

"Where are we taking them?" I asked as she handed me the other end of her wrist rope. We both tied the rope first before we picked up our signs. Mine I tied around my wrist, just tight enough to not fall off, but not tight enough that I couldn't get it off in a hurry.

"Well, you said we were near the boy's cabins, right?"

I nodded before whispering a brief affirmative.

"Then we are near the bathhouse which is near the mud trail Tyler trapped us in. We can ditch them upside down in the mud. Come on, Kayla told me a bit about the trails. I should be able to lead us the right way."

"You're brilliant," I said as I picked up my signs and followed her into the woods.

Our luck held as we made it unerringly to the muddy trail where we'd been trapped before. We felt the surface of the boards to see which side had the lettering before we placed them down to make makeshift walkways over the muddier areas. We easily made it through all six signs.

We had a brief laugh at one point as we saw the dim glow of a flashlight that was stuck under a thin layer of mud. Not wanting to pass up the opportunity for a light, we carefully turned it off and freed it from the mud. Judging by its feel, it was one of the heavy-duty flashlights. While we weren't sure it was waterproof, we decided to clean it off in a tiny stream anyway. Wendy remembered that the stream was just on the other side of the girl's cabins, so if we followed it, we'd find the cabins.

Sure enough, she was right.

We repeated the procedure with the girl's cabin signs and were back at the edge of the woods with no one the wiser. Only, this time, there was no pile of signs waiting for me as we made our escape. I waited until we were further into the darkness before asking Wendy about it.

"I hid them where they'll never find them," Wendy said. She giggled as she tied her rope back to her wrist. We'd taken it off so we could work separately to take down the signs.

"Where?" I asked as I also tied the rope back on.

"The stream," she said, her face beaming.

Wendy's cleverness never ceased to amaze me. As I thought of the signs floating down the stream with their ridiculous names, I couldn't help wondering who might discover them. Would a fisherman see a sign for a *House Cheer* or *Smiles*? Would a child wandering out to his local creek find one and wonder at the meaning of *Elation* and why someone would etch it onto a wooden board?

I chuckled as I thought of the possibilities, and when Wendy asked what I was thinking, I gladly told her. Then we both had a good, though quiet, laugh.

"Did you see the true names?" Wendy asked as we carefully found the trail we'd used.

"Yeah," I replied, sounding a bit smug, even to my own ears. I couldn't help feeling like I'd accomplished far more than the simple removal of a few false names. It felt invigorating to be liberating everyone from the harsh rules of Head Counselor Petrel and Teacher.

"I saw a few," Wendy said as she slowed her pace. "There was Tethys, Thea and uh…Mnemo…Mnemosyne? I'm not really sure how to pronounce that last one."

As Wendy pondered the last name's pronunciation, I couldn't help but ask if she thought the names were also of Greek Titans as Naython or his *brudder* Jiminy had said. I also shared the names I remembered from the boy's cabins.

"Oh! I bet they are!" Wendy agreed joyously. "I'd almost forgotten about that. It's so lame of them to have hidden such fun names. When I get out of here, I'm going to research them."

"I'm going to research what this place was before it was turned into this nightmare," I added.

"We'll have to share our research," Wendy said, and I agreed.

"Where to now?" she asked before I could ask her why she'd

been sent to this camp.

"Do you think you can lead us to…" I paused as I realized I was saying the plan out loud.

Wendy sighed and cupped a hadn't around her ear. I was glad it was so dark so she couldn't see me blushing as I leaned in to whisper, "Art barn."

CHAPTER FORTY-FIVE

Motion Sensor

Finding a clear path was difficult in the dark, and avoiding twigs was nearly impossible. Thankfully there were plenty of leaves and plants that helped cushion and silence most of our steps.

As far as I could tell, the adults were all keeping to the main camp trails, sidewalks, or the asphalt road that wound its way from the cabins to the entrance. We had our first real scare as headlights from a car illuminated the forest for a moment. After that, we only caught occasional glimpses of distant flashlights.

Wendy did a good job of leading us, despite how dark it was. Our going was slow, and we often risked using the flashlight, which we shielded under folded layers of my shirt. I was surprised it still worked, despite the mud and water bath it had received.

Luckily, we weren't far from the art barn as the girl's cabins were relatively close to the terrible place. Wendy tugged on the rope as we reached our destination. It felt like hours had passed since we'd begun our nighttime quest, though I had no idea how long it had actually been. I missed my phone. I was about to ask Wendy if she had hers, but if she had brought it on our night quest, then it had likely been lost to the mud or terminated by our swim.

Before either of us could move or say anything, a bright light, far brighter than the headlights had been, illuminated the area. We both froze as the white light lit up the night.

Ahead of us was the very well illuminated side of the Art Barn. An animal, roughly the size of a raccoon or maybe a skunk, scrambled across the open area and disappeared into a different section of the woods.

I don't know how long we both stood there before Wendy said, "Motion sensor."

We breathed a synchronized sigh of relief.

"Did we set it off, or did the animal?" I asked, mostly just to break the silence between us. It was creepy being out in the woods at night, and the sight of the Art Barn was bringing back bad memories of gray boxes and silence.

"Dunno, but what's your plan?"

I wasn't sure how to answer. My original plan, before Tyler had butted his way in, had been to disrupt the camp by causing a stir at breakfast, making life difficult for the counselors, and by finding a way to somehow disrupt Teacher's creation of the signs. What could I do against the wooden boards? Would they wash away down the river, same as the cabin names? Would that be enough? Teacher could always gather more wood, though. What if I took the tool he made to use them?

I smiled at Wendy as a wicked idea came to me. I finally knew what I had to do. I motioned for her to follow me. We were at the right of the barn and we needed to be at the front. She nodded in understanding, and we made our way to a slightly different game trail that led us to a secluded section of bushes near the front of the barn. I stopped us with three tugs on the rope as I saw a problem with my plan.

The barn doors were closed, a large chain bolted and locked around their handles. We weren't getting in, at least not that way.

"What's with the stools?" Wendy asked, breaking up my thoughts.

I chuckled as I realized she hadn't likely heard about Teacher removing them.

"Remember how they squeaked when we were there together?"

"Yeah."

"He had them removed because of us."

"Seriously? Wow."

We stared at the ridiculous scene for a moment longer, then I broke the silence. "I need to get in there," I whispered, hoping she might have a plan.

"Those doors are locked," Wendy whispered matter-of-factly.

She carefully looked around. "There's a backdoor, but it goes to a small shop. I don't think it's used anymore."

"How do you know that?" I whispered back.

"I saw it when Teacher had me sit out back, remember? But that's not the problem..." She gave me a pleading look.

"What?"

"*Spiders*."

I didn't know how to respond to that. I wasn't a fan of the eight-legged critters, but Wendy looked like she was on the verge of tears, and I didn't know how to respond to that. "What if I go?" I suggested. We'd already passed the back of the place, or I assumed we had since we'd come from that direction. I hadn't seen any spiders or felt their webs then, but I hadn't been looking for them either.

"Then what do I do?"

"Keep lookout?"

"What, and caw like a bird if someone comes?"

She had a point. There weren't many sounds someone could make that wouldn't be suspicious, particularly nocturnal ones. Hooting like an owl came to mind, but I wasn't sure what that would sound like, and it seemed like a bad idea to go testing sounds now while we were still trying to avoid catching anyone's attention.

My eyes wandered to the ground as I thought. Then I had a brilliant idea as I spotted what looked like an acorn, though the lighting wasn't the best for me to be sure. Acting more confident than I felt, I picked it up. Luckily, it was just a regular acorn and not some spider sac.

"If someone comes, toss this on the roof or a window," I said, handing over the acorn.

"What now?" she asked as she took it.

"I'm going to make my way to the back." I began untying the rope so I could move freely again. "Hopefully, there's a way in and I can do something about those stupid signs."

Wendy smiled. "Good plan. I'll follow behind you for a bit."

We nodded foolishly at each other, then we both broke out in stupid grins. I knew I had never done anything so foolish before or so meaningful, and I felt Wendy must have been thinking the same thing. At long last, we were going to bring the camp down!

CHAPTER FORTY-SIX

On

Now that Wendy had reminded me of the spiders, I started seeing signs of the rotten things everywhere. I also noticed something else. The back of the barn wasn't illuminated like the front. Either that meant it had its own motion sensor or it didn't have one at all. While that meant I would have a difficult time avoiding webs, it did mean I would avoid being easily spotted should a counselor come by.

I heard the footsteps go silent behind me, and I knew that Wendy had stopped following. With more webbing and a few spiders resting boldly in the middle of their webs, I didn't blame her for refusing to go further. I went back for her.

"You should stay here," I whispered as Wendy hesitantly came closer. "Here," I said, handing her the flashlight. "Just in case."

She gave a half smile as she accepted it and hid it under her shirt. "Good luck," she whispered as I took off.

Getting out of the tree line was more difficult than I thought it would be. There really were webs everywhere. Someone had to go, though, and I wasn't about to have Wendy make the attempt. My resolve wavered as a spider skittered across my neck. Then the light went out.

I gritted my teeth and hummed to keep from swearing, like I'd heard my mom do. I'd nearly reached the backdoor. I was so *close*! Why did the light have to go off now?

I debated stumbling ahead blindly. I'd seen the path only moments before. If I was careful, there was a chance I could follow it, despite losing my night vision. My memory wasn't so good. As I stumbled, I decided to wait for my night vision to come back before attempting to move again. It wouldn't do any good to rush things now and risk alerting a counselor.

As I waited, I began thinking more about the counselors and why they hadn't come running when the light had gone off on the barn. There was no way they hadn't seen it. Unless, were they on their way now? If they were, then he was running out of time to execute his plan, and all for night vision that could be ruined if another animal went running back across the open area in front of the barn.

More than a few twigs snapped under my feet as I pressed forward, and more than a few spiderwebs made contact. I barely noticed that I'd made it to an open area, but when I did notice, I quickly did a rub down to remove any unwanted tagalongs. Even though it was dark, standing in an open area had me on edge. I quickly moved for what I thought was the door I'd seen before.

It was locked, but as I held the handle, something jabbed my wrist. I flinched as I feared some nasty spider had bitten me, but my wrist was fine. I reached out again and found what I'd felt before, cold metal, a key in the lock. I shook my head in relieved disbelief.

It took a bit of wiggling to get the key to work, but eventually the thing turned enough for the door to unlock. As I opened the door, I noticed a definite lack of squeaking or creaking. At least that much had gone my way.

While the door didn't creak, I was at a disadvantage as I realized the darkness inside the barn was far greater than the darkness outside. I suddenly regretted giving Wendy the flashlight. I stepped back and looked for where I thought she might be, but even though my night vision had returned enough, it wasn't strong enough to see through the dense darkness of the trees and undergrowth.

A twig snapped, and I jumped. The sound came from the front of the barn and not where Wendy should have been. I ducked back inside the room and debated closing the door, but I didn't want to risk it suddenly deciding to be loud and screech shut. As I stood waiting in the dark, I wondered why Wendy hadn't alerted me with an acorn, rock, or something on the metal roof. Unless she'd seen that it was an animal, like the one from before?

The light at the front of the barn turned on again, and with its renewed light, I could see more of the room I was in from a window in the room, a window that led into the main part of the barn. I used the light to walk over to it, but I had to stand on my tiptoes to see into the barn. The light, I could see, was coming from a gap in the front doors. It was all I needed.

I could see clearly enough now to make out tables and utensils, and more importantly, Teacher's workstation with the boards and tools. I debated running out and seeing what had tripped the light or going ahead with the plan. Since Wendy hadn't thrown a rock or acorn, I decided it must be safe enough to continue.

Moving quickly, and still keeping an ear out for anything against the roof of the barn, I worked on forcing the window open. It creaked painfully loud, but it did open. Adrenaline pumping, I flung myself up and through the opening. I bumped my head as I landed on the other side, but I had no time to worry about that.

My head ringing and my blood pumping, I rushed over to the workbench and began searching the table for Teacher's wood burner. Without that, he wouldn't have the tools needed to burn names into the wood. I found it easily enough, but then I saw something else. There were paintbrushes and paint cans on the workbench. Even if I took the burner, Teacher would still have the means to make more words forbidden.

My shoulders slumped as I realized another flaw with my logic. Even with his tools gone, what would stop him from using camp funds to buy more tools or boards? My plan was falling apart.

I looked at the burner in my hand. Something *had* to be done.

A new idea formed. It was risky, totally dangerous, and very reckless. It was also pretty illegal, but I didn't let myself think about that. Drastic times called for drastic measures.

Moving faster than before, I arranged the wood planks in a stacked formation that allowed air flow between the planks. That done, I opened different cabinets and searched for paper, which I found with little trouble. Then I stuffed the empty sections between the wood planks and around the table.

That done, I worked by feel to get the burner plugged in. My finger snagged on a sharp edge as I cut my finger. I silently cursed my rotten luck and stuck my finger in my mouth. With my other hand, I took the unknown tool off its hook and looked it over. It was a wire cutter.

I was about to put it back on its peg when another idea came to mind. I took the tools and pocketed them for later. Then I turned my attention back to the burner. My time with the light, I feared, was running out. With my uninjured hand, I located a socket and plugged the wood burner in. I was rewarded as a red *on* light came to life.

There was no time to wait for it to warm up. I used the light from the crack in the doors to locate the temperature gauge. Then I turned the knob to its highest setting and left it heating up on a stack of papers, which led to the pile of boards.

I regretted angering Teacher with the stools as I struggled to make my clumsy escape out the window. I hit my head on a wood panel as I fell out through the window. Something tore my shorts and something else snagged my shirt. I didn't want to imagine the size of the nails no doubt poking out of boards or the tetanus I had no doubt narrowly avoided. I stood up as quickly as I dared and fumbled to close the window.

It moaned and creaked as I forced it shut. I sighed with relief as I peered once more through the closed glass. The light at the front of the barn went out again, and I was left in darkness, but it didn't matter. I'd done it!

In the near darkness, I made out the red light of hope, and more importantly, I thought I could see the faint red glow of the tool as it pressed against the paper. With a foolish grin, I left and closed the door. I was even clever enough to lock it behind me and take the key, in case fingerprints ever became an issue.

Now all that was left was to get to Wendy and then get as far away from here as possible. My thoughts were disrupted as something struck the metal roof with a tiny clang. My adrenaline going once more, I dashed into the cover of the trees.

CHAPTER FORTY-SEVEN

Retreat

Web after web smacked me in the face as I made my mad dash into the tree line. After feeling tiny legs scampering over my exposed face and arms, I stopped and focused instead on slapping away whatever clung to me. I didn't care if I was caught, I just wanted to be free of the things!

I was nearly done clearing off the worst of it when something small struck me in the arm. I turned and saw the dark outline of Wendy. She was pointing desperately in the direction of the front of the barn. I picked my path carefully and made my way to her as fast as I dared. She grabbed my hand and I realized she needed my help in guiding her. Without the barn's light, she likely didn't have very good night vision anymore.

Then what had upset her?

I moved us both to the side of the barn. With a sense of dread, I saw what had upset her. Three sets of flashlights were moving along the sidewalk toward the barn and fast. We had to leave the area immediately.

Now that I had the wire cutters, there was no reason to stick around. I tapped Wendy's arm to get her attention. Then I cupped my hands and whispered, "Rock tower."

She frowned, but then she handed me the rope and we set off down a worn path. By the time we were on our way down a hill, the motion sensor for the Art Barn went off again. This time, it was the counselors who had triggered it.

We stumbled down the hill and disappeared in the darkness.

There was no time to worry about my actions in the barn, but when my foot slipped in a small puddle of mud at the base of the hill, I stopped Wendy and held out the key I'd taken.

"What is it?" she whispered urgently.

"Evidence," I said glumly. I motioned that I wanted to bury it in the mud, but she took it from me instead.

"Better idea," she said with a wink.

Then we were off again. We didn't encounter any lights or see any more counselors as we made swift progress away from the Art Barn. Suddenly, Wendy gave three unexpected tugs on the rope and I stopped. I was about to ask her what was going on, but she held a finger up to her lips, or that's what I thought I saw. It was too dark to see that clearly.

She came over and untied my wrist. Then she pulled out the key, squeezed my arm, and wandered off. I wasn't sure what to do. I was even more confused by her emphasis on staying quiet, as though I wasn't already aware of that.

One thing was clear, I couldn't see her anymore. I had to trust her. As I stood in the dark, I listened for any sound of pursuit from the three counselors we'd seen at the barn. If we had been too loud, then they were sure to be after us.

Just as my paranoia had me thinking the counselors had found me and were sneaking up on me, Wendy reappeared. She flipped the flashlight on, and it lit up the area just enough for us to make out the other's face, but only just barely. Wendy was grinning mischievously. When I tried to silently ask her about the key, she gave me an elaborate wink. It had to be elaborate for me to see it, and I chuckled quietly at that. Then she held her finger to her lips again, and I realized that she had been serious before about being quiet here. I nodded even though I didn't understand.

She gave me the rope back and we started off again. I quickly noticed that our going was much slower. A moment later, I realized why. Across our path, just a foot off the ground, a rope was stretched across the path. Wendy pointed it out a moment later, and I looked up in concern.

I heard her sigh as she undid the flashlight enough for me to see what was going on. All around us were ropes, logs, some old tires, and a few other things that I couldn't identify in the dark. She shielded the light back to its previous level before I could see everything.

I nodded as I realized we were at the rope course that Kayla had talked about finding.

Travel here was slow going as we had to look out for obstacles that were meant for daylight usage. The more we weaved or lifted our feet obnoxiously high to take a step, the more I thought about why Wendy had silenced me. Then I remembered that the nurse's office had been bugged. I cringed as I realized the Art Barn had also likely been bugged. At least if there were cameras, the interior had been too dark to see me, or so I hoped. I was, however, glad I hadn't spoken aloud. Maybe they'd blame the noise I'd made falling or opening the window on an animal. I could hope.

Regardless, the appearance of counselors at the Art Barn so soon after I'd made a ruckus made Wendy's caution at the rope course area understandable. Who knew what parts of camp were or were not under surveillance?

After leaving the rope course, travel went much faster. It went so much faster, that I wondered how we had ever made it through the tediously slow pace before. Wendy made a few errors on this latest trail, but I didn't care. My spirits were high. We had accomplished so much. Even if my plans failed, we'd left our mark on this place. I was sure of it. Besides, if Naython and Jiminy made it out, then Tyler's scheme could still work, just not in the way he'd intended.

My spirits were still high as Wendy brought us to the back of the rock tower. I stepped out into the open and took the rope of my wrist for what I felt was likely the last time. The coolness of the night air felt refreshing. Everything felt like it was going my way. I'd felt so crushed by the constant rules and the constant badgering of the counselors that I didn't care if that feeling was unrealistic. It felt nice to be making a difference.

Wendy tugged my arm, and as I saw her face, that feeling disappeared.

"What is it?" I asked.

She pointed in the direction we'd come, and I saw what had her so horrified. On the top of a hill, I saw the unmistakable white flash of a counselor's flashlight. Either we were being followed, or they were walking the trails. One way or another, our adventure was coming to an end.

CHAPTER FORTY-EIGHT

Climbing Tower

With the counselors hot on our trail, I rushed toward the tower. I knew the locks were on the other side for the climbing portion of the tower, but seeing a door on the back, I went for it instead. I heard Wendy following behind me, and when I had trouble finding the lock on the door, she came to my aid with the flashlight. Its muted light wasn't great, but it was enough. Once I had the lock located, I used the wire cutter tool I'd taken from the Art Barn to cut it. Unfortunately, the lock was too thick and wouldn't be cut, but the thin chains it held gave way easily enough.

Together, we carefully unwound the chain as quietly as we could. I was glad we weren't on the other side of the tower as we would have been more exposed by the empty field, but with the counselors on the trail behind us, I still felt overly nervous. The sound of dogs off in the distance didn't help either. I thought we had left them behind. Judging by the nervous way Wendy kept looking around, she likely thought so too.

As we carefully put the chain on the ground, I kept my eye on the door. After being at the barn with all the webs, I happily noted the lack of spider webs. Hopefully the inside would be the same.

When I opened the door, a flash of bright light temporarily blinded me. I don't know how either of us kept from screaming, but I know I jumped.

"Get in," Wendy hissed as she recovered first.

I rubbed my eyes and she grabbed me by the elbow and pulled me into the climbing tower with her. As the door swung shut, I saw

Wendy pointing up at the bright light that had surprised us. It was another motion sensor, but unlike the one at the barn, this one was inside rather than out.

I nodded to show I understood what had happened. Then, I held up a finger to my lips as I recalled the potential for the camp being bugged, and Wendy rolled her eyes at the annoyance of not being able to talk freely. I shrugged as I turned around, not the least bit surprised by anything annoying the camp could do at this point. There was a simple latch on the door, and I used it to keep the thing shut. It wasn't designed to keep anyone from getting in, but it would at least prevent the door from swinging open and lighting up the area again.

Now that we were inside, I noticed that the room we were in was in much better upkeep than the outside of the tower. The floor was concrete, and the walls were clean and clear of webbing. The cleanliness only made me feel more confident about the room being bugged.

Wendy saw me looking around and pointed around the room. There were harnesses, rope, helmets, and a slew of other rock-climbing equipment. There was also a maintenance ladder.

By the time we'd finished looking around, we were both smiling and looking up a latch that no doubt opened out onto the roof of the tower. While we were both in silent agreement on where to go next, we weren't in agreement on how to get there. When I immediately went to climb the ladder, she hummed disapprovingly.

When I stopped climbing and looked back, she was busy pulling a harness off its hooks. I debated going up anyway, but I changed my mind as I saw the height of the tower. Wendy's idea of using the harnesses and the hooks attached to them made more sense than making the climb without them.

We took turns helping each other with the harnesses. It didn't help that we were both nervously watching the door and not paying full attention to what we were doing. Those counselors were still out there, and the light from the tower had likely been easily seen.

It took several tries to get our harnesses on, and I don't think either of us felt particularly confident that we had them on properly. Still, it was safer than before. We used the clasps to latch onto the metal ladder and began our climb. When I reached the top rungs, I stopped as I had to work on unlocking the latch. In the end, I had to use the wire cutters to get it open, and I only barely made it in time as the light below us went out.

"We took too long," Wendy whispered from lower down on the ladder.

I shrugged, and when I realized she couldn't see that in the dark, I decided to open the hatch and let us out. Once outside again, it was easier to see. There was railing on three of the tower's walls, so there was little risk of falling off, even without the harnesses. There was also little risk of being seen.

I helped Wendy up next and fumbled to close the hatch behind her. It was too dark for me to see very well, but I knew my eyes would adjust soon. Wendy was the one who found a security wire that went around the tower's perimeter and attached our claw-like clips to it.

"How did you do that?" I whispered in admiration of her speed in the dark.

"Do what?"

"See. How did you see? I was blind after that light went out."

"Oh, that's easy. I knew my eyes would have to adjust, so I closed one of them on the way up. I read about it in a pirate book once. That's what eye patches were for. Or at least, that's what they were for when you didn't lose an eye," she said with a brief giggle.

"Pirate," I said, bemused by the whole idea.

Wendy giggled again. We sat there and enjoyed a cool breeze. We might've sat there forever if we hadn't heard dogs barking near-by.

"Trouble," Wendy said. As she spoke, she inched closer to the edge for a look at the ground around the tower.

"Best spot to keep lookout," I replied as I looked over the edge.

"Agreed. What do you think will happen now?"

"Camp will be closed," I said smugly. "There's no way it won't. Campers went missing, and well, it just *can't* stay open," I said elusively.

"Do you think they saw the light?" Wendy asked, eyeing the area around the tower nervously.

"Don't know. We should probably keep whispering though. Even if this place isn't bugged, the sound of our voices might reach them."

"Good point," Wendy whispered back. "Hey, what's that?" she asked a moment later.

CHAPTER FORTY-NINE

Fire

Off in the distance, where the art barn should have been, an orange glow lit up the night. I hadn't expected for there to be so much light from a fire. On the ground, I saw three flashlights weaving between trees. At first, I wasn't sure if they were coming for the tower, away and toward the barn, or if they were lost. The lights kept dancing around in different directions, but then I remembered the rope course and laughed.

"What's so funny?" Wendy asked, a hardness to her voice I hadn't heard before.

I pointed at the flashlights. "They're stuck in the rope course. You must've led us through really well, considering they have their lights unshielded and are lost."

"Oh, sorry. I thought you were laughing at the fire. Yeah, they do look lost. But, Daniel," she was looking at the burning building as she spoke.

"Teacher must've left his tools on," I said very carefully. If there were any hidden recording devices, I wasn't about to blurt out the truth. And this way, there'd be a case against Teacher.

I could tell by the look she gave me that she didn't believe that Teacher had left a tool on. I wasn't sure what she was thinking, and as the silence grew, I started to worry that I had gone too far.

"*Teacher's* negligence will likely cost this camp greatly," she said, emphasizing Teacher's name.

I bit my tongue to keep from sighing with relief.

"Though," she continued, her tone suddenly harsher, "it would be a great shame if any animals were harmed in the fire."

"You saw the inside of that place, it was clean. Besides, I'm sure that if there were any animals that were smart enough to get in, they would be smart enough to get out."

"That's true," she said, her tone less harsh.

Again, I had to keep from sighing with relief. I honestly hadn't thought of the surrounding area when I'd set the fire. Wendy wasn't wrong. I should have thought that plan through.

"At least this means the counselors won't have time to chase us down," I said, no longer feeling confident about the fire.

As if to accentuate my point, the lights in the trees all turned toward the Art Barn. I saw them a few times through the trees, but not as easily as I had when they'd been moving around the rope course.

A siren went off in the distance, jarring me out of my guilty thoughts. Far off, I thought I heard the sound of a fire truck.

"Well, at least they should be here soon," Wendy said, sounding as relieved as I felt. "I still don't know if I like it," she said, slowly, "but I can appreciate the benefit of it."

I smiled lamely. With the potential risk to the forested area and the animals, I wasn't really up for celebrating anymore.

"You know, I never told you why I was here," she said, drawing me out of my depression.

"Oh?" She had my attention, but when I looked over, she seemed to regret bringing up the topic. I hated to think how pathetic I must've looked for her to want to talk about something she clearly didn't want to talk about. "It's alright, you don't have to tell me," I said.

She shook her head and shifted as she tried shifting into a more comfortable position, which wasn't easy in the harnesses. When she was comfortable, she began.

"My parents don't even know this, but I'm bullied at school. Most of the teacher's turn a blind eye, at least they do until I strike back. I've never used my fists, but I know how to use words." She paused for a bit, as though struggling with an unpleasant memory. "There's one teacher, he's cruel; he actually *encourages* one of the boys to hit me."

"What?! That can't be! You have to tell your parents."

"It is true. And I can't. They have enough problems, if similar ones, in the places they work. It's a good school. If I can get through it, I'll be better off than most."

"That isn't right," I argued, feeling more perplexed than ever. "Why are they picking on you anyway? You're so clever and smart!"

Wendy smiled, but it was a sad smile. "It's the way I look," she said slowly.

"What's wrong with the way you look?" I couldn't recall there being anything weird or odd with how she looked, and it was too dark to try looking now. "You look fine to me, and I don't think you look any different now, except your clothes are probably still a bit wet like mine." She smiled as I spoke. It was a happier smile now, at least.

"You mean it, don't you? It's not the way I dress," she said slowly. "It's my skin color."

It took me a moment to recover. I had thought racism was done with. "What's wrong with that? So, what if you have dark skin? Lots of people do. You're so clever and intelligent. You make the counselors trip all over themselves, it's great! How can they not see how great you are?"

Wendy sniffled, and I shut my mouth. I wasn't sure if I was making things better or worse.

"Can we maybe talk about something else," she suggested quietly.

It was so unlike her to be doubtful, so I did my best to come up with something else to talk about. "How did you know about the bully, the girl at school, and about me?" I regretted the question immediately. My mind went blank before I could come up with a better topic.

She was silent for a while before finally saying, "You really don't know, do you?"

"Know what?" I shifted a little, feeling nervous about the question.

"I'm not sure... What I mean to say is... Do you know Abigail?"

"Uh..." It took me a few seconds to remember her. "You mean the *really* shy girl?"

"Yes, but do you recognize her from anywhere?"

I frowned and tried to remember, but nothing came up. I shrugged.

"Wow. I'm not sure if I'm more impressed or upset with you right now."

"What did I do?" I protested.

"Abigail's the girl you defended at school, you dolt! She's in *your* class!" Wendy shook her head. "It's impressive you would stand up for someone you don't know. But how could you not recognize her?"

I desperately wanted the topic to drop. How could I be expected to remember that? "I hadn't really met her when I heard Adrian picking on her. I just did what I thought was right and stood up to the guy."

The fire truck had reached the camp gates and the noise was enough to distract us both from the conversation. There was another noise I thought I heard as well.

"Helicopter," Wendy said, pointing at a light in the sky.

"They brought a helicopter for the fire?" I asked, feeling even more guilty than I had before. The helicopter reached the camp around the time the truck reached the burning barn. I thought I caught a glimpse of a stream of water hitting the smoking, burning building, but I couldn't be sure. I only hoped the fire wouldn't spread.

My night vision was lost again as a bright light beamed down on us from the air. The noise of the helicopter, so close overhead, made talking difficult with Wendy.

"Looks like they know we're here!" she shouted, drawing me out of my thoughts.

"You think?" I asked sarcastically.

"Take a look," she said, pointing at a group of people, flashlights, and dogs that were making their way into the clearing of the kickball field.

"Oh," I said. I hadn't realized we'd been spotted by those on the ground and in the air.

"What?" she shouted as I'd forgotten to.

"Guess we can't hide now," I shouted back.

CHAPTER FIFTY

Caught

The helicopter moved off, leaving us to our thoughts.

"Do you think they're going after those other two?" Wendy asked.

"Maybe," I said in my normal tone of voice. I thought about going back to a whisper, but it seemed pointless now. "I never got a chance to ask all the questions I wanted to," I complained as I realized it was over and that I'd wasted so much time.

Wendy giggled. "We aren't' caught yet! What did you want to know?"

"I don't know. Just more about you. What books you read, which must be awesome if you knew that eyepatch trick. How you kept being one step ahead. I don't know."

"Well," she began, "I read fantasy books, some science fiction, and lots of mystery books. As for how I kept one step ahead, that's easy. The restrooms all had writing on the walls from previous campers. If you knew where to look, you could find out different things about their time here."

"For real?" I asked, my mind blown.

"Of course! Some of us even left our own messages on the walls."

From the way she smiled, I knew she'd been one of the girls to leave a message to future campers. The group of officers, dogs, and counselors would be here soon, but I did my best to keep my eyes on Wendy and my mind off the consequences of our attempted escape.

"The Bathhouse," Wendy continued, "was also a great place to spread word as different girls from different groups would often meet up there to use the restroom. The counselors couldn't tell us not to pee, so we had the perfect excuses to leave the groups. That's actually where Abigail told me about you. There was even a sad message about a boy named Ty and how he'd been trapped here for three weeks."

"Yikes."

"Yeah, I'm pretty sure now that was Tyler."

"Never mind," I said, no longer feeling guilty for that traitor.

She chuckled. "Someone found a message that claimed they'd found Teacher's true name and that saying it would be a way to break the rules without breaking the rules."

"Because his name was similar to forbidden words?" I asked.

"Exactly, but now I'm not so sure that it wasn't a trap. It would make sense for the counselors to leave up the graffiti if it meant locating troublemakers. That's what I think nearly happened to Kayla. She'd found the message and gone off in search of answers in Head Counselor Petrel's office."

"Seriously? She really doesn't like sticking with the group," I said, recalling the time she'd abandoned us on the kickball field.

Wendy laughed. "But she does find out some good information!" she said, defending her friend. "Anyway, she hadn't returned for dinner, and just as a counselor began suspiciously counting the members in my group, well, that's when I stood up to taunt Teacher. It kept her absence from being discovered, though it did cost me a terrible visit to see Mr. Petrel. He was so full of himself. In the end, I still don't know if Creton Maleficus was Teacher's real name. Kayla found it in the files, but she said it had been too easy. Considering the different traps they seemed to set for us, I have my doubts as well."

"It would be pretty awesome if it was his real name, though."

"Yeah," she said with a smile.

"Oh!" I said, an idea striking me suddenly. I pulled the tiny pencil that I'd been carrying around most of the day out of my pocket. It was a bit wet, but I was sure it would still write. "Do you still have the flashlight?" I asked.

"Yeah, but it looks like they've reached the door," she said, looking down at the group of people and dogs. The dogs were barking excitedly, and the officers didn't look too pleased, at least that's what I thought I saw. The lighting wasn't the best.

The flashlight clicked on and I began to write furiously. I wrote my full name and an email I used.

"Swap," Wendy said, handing me the flashlight.

We swapped flashlight for pencil and I did my best to memorize her email. It was easy enough, but I didn't want to forget. Then she added something else, *Deny everything.*

"Do you have it memorized?" she asked innocently, and when I nodded, she began erasing the information. I pulled the wire cutters back out and looked around. They were the only thing that could link me back to the barn.

Wendy poked me and when I looked, she pointed down at a new message: *Leave them and never talk about them.* Then she erased that too.

Someone banged on the ladder that led up to our hideout and I heard a loud screech as someone pulled out a megaphone.

"We know you're up there," someone called out, their voice calm and soothing. Clearly, they'd had practice. "We're not mad. We just want you to come down safely and get you home to your parents. We're going to send an officer up to help get you down safe, is that alright with you?"

We looked at each other and shrugged. We had no intention of jumping, if that was what they were worried about. I looked over the railing and the guy seemed to panic.

"We'll come down!" I shouted back.

"Uh, please wait for the officer!" he called back, but it was too late. I'd already opened the hatch and swapped my clasps from the safety wire over to the ladder. Wendy quickly did the same.

"We're probably better prepared for this than they are," she said as she worked.

Now that the hatch was open, there was plenty of light for us to see as someone had triggered the motion sensor in the room below. As I looked down, I saw two officers struggling to put on harnesses.

"Do you think they know those sizes are for kids?" I asked, noticing that the officers were putting on the smaller harnesses.

Wendy giggled.

The first officer to greet us was Kevin's father. Far from being angry, annoyed, upset, or any of the other emotions I had anticipated facing, the officer was practically beaming with joy.

"Thank you," he said, his voice full of gratitude. "Now, keep quiet," he cautioned us, his voice barely above a whisper. "and wait for a lawyer before saying *anything*," he advised. Then he raised his voice as he said, "I have the two stray campers. They're safe. If you could please alert their parents, Officer Hays."

After that, we were handed over to Officer Hays. She didn't say much as we were escorted to the front of the camp. Just as I thought we were going to be allowed to wait for our parents together, we were separated.

"Don't worry," Officer Hays said, "Your parents are on the way."

"What's going to happen to this place?" I asked.

"It's going to be under severe investigation and will likely be closed. I would highly recommend waiting for a lawyer before talking, however," she cautioned, just as Kevin's father had cautioned earlier.

Then, it was my turn to reunite with my parents. There was a lot of emotion involved in that meeting, but I kept quiet. It wasn't that I wanted to punish them, but I took the officers' advice and kept quiet.

As time passed, my parents did the same silent treatment to me. I had only been quiet one night, but as the weeks went by, they kept quiet about anything concerning the camp. They also monitored my online activity to the point that the only message I was able to send to Wendy was that I wasn't sure if I'd be able to send her any messages. I hated being right.

My only hope in making contact again lay in the new school year. I held out hope that the girl's network would remain strong, even outside of camp. I had to hope that Abigail would be at school this year and that maybe she'd have news on Wendy and the camp.

Epilogue

The first day of school went by agonizingly slow. Abigail still went to the same school, but I had difficulty getting close enough to talk to her. She disappeared during lunch and was nowhere to be found during recess. The girls all refused to talk to me, though they were more than happy to titter and imply I had a crush on Abigail.

As the final bell rang, I hesitated to stand. I'd been waiting all summer for a chance to talk to Abigail and to learn Wendy's and the camp's fate. My feet dragged as I collected my things and thought about the best way to find the shy girl. Despite my attempts to find her, it was Abigail who found me.

"I don't know what you said or what you did, but all I've heard all day is how you have a crush on me. That had better not be true!" Abigail glowered as she confronted me.

My jaw dropped and I had to look her over to make sure she was the same shy girl I'd met in camp. She looked like the same girl, but she didn't act the same! What had happened to the shy girl who could barely speak? The girl who spoke so softly as to barely be heard? The girl who couldn't make eye contact? This Abigail spoke clearly, loudly, and made darn sure to make eye contact!

"Abigail?" I asked hesitantly.

"Who else could it be?" Kayla said, coming up to stand beside her friend.

"You're here too?!" I cried out excitedly. I remembered the two girls had been friends at camp, but I'd never made the connection that they had known each other from school. I was glad Wendy wasn't here to see this.

"His brain's been addled from a day of studying instead of mischief making," Kayla teased. "Hey, do you flinch every time someone says teacher?" Kayla said, suddenly turning serious. "I do. Every time someone says teacher, I always picture *him*. Ugh, it's just awful."

"I want an answer," Abigail said sternly, as she did her best to ignore Kayla's rambling. Even so, she did flinch each time her friend said teacher.

"To what?" I asked, my own mind drifting to thoughts of Teacher.

"Do you have a crush on me?" Abigail glared and folded her arms across her chest.

"No," I said truthfully. "I've been looking for you all day though," I rushed on as Abigail looked suspicious. "Is the...uh... girls' network still...how's Wendy?"

Abigail sighed with relief while Kayla laughed.

"I'd hardly call it a network," Kayla said with an eye roll. "We just keep in touch is all."

"You're lucky then," I said, sounding as bitter as I felt.

Kayla laughed again, but Abigail looked serious once more. "I do have something for you," she said, sounding more like her old self. She carefully took a vanilla envelope out of her backpack. "It's from Wendy," she said softly.

"Come on," Kayla said as she half pushed and half pulled Abigail after her. "He has some catching up to do."

I hardly noticed as the two girls left me alone in the classroom. I reverently opened the vanilla envelope and peered inside. There was something dark at the bottom, and I pulled that out first. It was the key to the Art Barn, the one Wendy'd taken and hidden for me. I couldn't believe she'd retrieved it!

Next, I pulled out newspaper clippings along with several typed notes. Most of the notes were written to Abigail, Kayla, or to some unknown group. I assumed the last one to be the girls' network.

There was one unopened envelope, which I pulled out last. In it was a handwritten letter from Wendy.

Hello again, Danie! I hope the rest of your summer went well. I'm just glad to be done answerng those ame questions over and over again with he police. Did thy make you do that too? Not that it mattered. They did't listen to us, not a one!! How do I know? Loo at the newspaper clippings. They've gon and coered it up! All of t. Including...well, icluding some things that are probably bet let covered up.

They got way with everyhing! But tat's not the odd part. The counslors, where they ae mentioned, have different names. hen I checked the names, they came up as ded people, like really long dead people. There's a library near me with a great Genealogy department. The librarian were the ones that helped me track down the people, or rather their names. This leads me to assume they were using the names of dead people instead of their real ones. How creepy!

That isn't even the oddest part! asically, the whole thing was pinned on psychiatrist Hilton. All the articles, if you'll look at them eal close, are consistent on both the name and on the gult. THEY NEVER GOT NURSE PAM'S NAME RIGHT! And where does the Hilton come from? Her last name? I haven't been ale to find her anywher either. Not a false name or otherwise.

The odest part is, psychiatrist Hilton is referred to as a he (again consistently) and they say the whole positivity cap was his pet project.. We were part of an unwitting study n human behavio. Sevral counselors confessed to being branwashed on the experimet or study. Where it gets odd is that while Pam is never mentioned, a nurse is mentioned in just one article. Odder still, Teacher and Mr. Petrel are never mentioned and there are no photos of them, but there are photos o the other counselors. (Thse are rare as individual photos, but I did find a group shot. Someone came forward and said an upset parent had demanded a camp photo with counselors and campers. Hence hat phot.)

Did I mention the camp was closed? Well, it is. It's losed up tight and there are several For Sale signs and postings. I've included sme newspaper clippings on it too.

I wish I had ore news to give you, particularly good

*news, but this is all the research I've managed to collect,
with help of course. If I learn more, I'll pass the news
along through the girls. They aren't the only ones looking into this. Whatever the truth is, you can be sure the
real investigation continus!!*

I read and re-read the letter before I realized I really needed to
get going or I'd make my father upset for making him wait. I tidied
up the envelope and all its contents and rushed outside. On the way
home, I thought about the letter over and over. The more I thought
about it, the more annoyed I became by the unusual number of spelling mistakes, particularly for someone as smart as Wendy. The more
I thought about it, the more I wondered if there was a hidden message. Wendy *was* clever after all, and she loved mystery novels.

The rest of the day, I did my best to behave and not draw attention to myself. Then, that night, when I finally had some free time
alone from my parents, I delved into the packet and checked to see
if the spelling errors were a mistake or a code. I wasn't disappointed.

Listen! Kevins father was bribed. More info to come!

More curious than ever, I delved into more of the packets and
found a different letter addressed to Kayla. Again, I found a hidden
message.

*I don't know what happened at camp. The news didn't get it right.
Stay in touch. Wendy.*

Letter after letter, I read through them all until I found all the
secrets. I learned that a million questions kid and his brother had
escaped to their mother's, which had caused an uproar from parents.
I also gained information on many of the campers and ways to keep
in touch online, though that message also cautioned against posting
anything sensitive or that our parents might be overly curious about.

A few letters in, I read that Kevin's father hadn't been bribed
exactly but that his son had been threatened and he'd been forced to
overlook the strange things happening at the camp. That explained
why he had thanked us at the tower. We'd likely given him and his
son a way out of the camp, what with the fire making camp undeniably unsafe. Then, with the missing kids, it must have been an easy
thing to shut the place down.

It took a month before I received a new packet with more letters,
hidden messages, and a final warning. Wendy's final message was

clear: *The research ends. Delving has caused families problems. The police know. Further investigation means further prosecution. Arson. No choice. Silence must prevail.*

Either they stop looking into the camp, or bad things would happen. It wasn't fair, but I wasn't about to risk anyone else just to find out what the camp had really been up to. It was one thing to have myself blamed for arson, but the idea of anyone else taking the fall didn't sit well with me, and that was the type of move Teacher and Mr. Petrel would have made just to keep everything quiet.

Despite the unfortunate conclusion, the hidden message had been hopeful and suggested meeting in person. It also gave an address, a number, and a new way to contact her online. Silence would prevail but not the way the police wanted. They'd stop leaving a paper trail, that was all.

I wasn't sure if Wendy meant for me to burn the evidence or not, but I followed the final instruction and burned the evidence packets later that night in a firepit outside my home. Then I posted a message online about it being a great night for a fire. Soon after, others from the camp posted similar fires and similar messages. Even Wendy posted a photo of her outside with a fire.

One of her friends commented with a familiar screenshot taken from a popular movie. I immediately recognized it as a beacon of Gondor. I smiled, knowing the next time any of the survivors of Camp Positivity had news, we could light the beacons and our forces would rally.

Characters & Pronunciation Guide

<u>Abigail (a′big′āl):</u> *Extremely* shy. She makes friends with Meliah, the less shy girl. She's in Counselor Kimberly's Home Group.

<u>Brennan (bren·nan):</u> He is nervous about everything. He is bunked in *House Joy* and is part of Counselor Delilah's Home Group.

<u>Brent (brent):</u> A kid who sat in the front row of Counselor Kimberly's Nature Walk class. He is part of Counselor Delilah's Home Group.

<u>Brian (brī·an):</u> A kid who joined Daniel in punishment in the nurse's office. Originally part of Counselor Melinda's home group. He is later forced to go with Daniel to Counselor Dave's Home Group before later being told to join Counselor Delilah's Home Group.

<u>Chelsea (chel·sē):</u> Part of Counselor Dave's Home Group.

<u>Coach Tammy (kōch tā′m′ē):</u> Punctuality is everything. Doesn't like rulebreakers.

<u>Counselor Delilah (koun′səl lər di lī′lə):</u> She later becomes Daniel's Home Group Counselor.

<u>Counselor Kimberly (koun′səl lər kim bur′lē):</u> The counselor who stops being seen after an incident at the Nature Center. Counselor to *House Glee*.

Counselor Dave (koun´səl lər dā´v): Also known as Mr. Chipper. He does not do well with criticism. He's cabin counselor to *House Jubilant*.

Counselor Emily (koun´səl lər em´i·lē): She is typically located near the sign and around the nurse's office. Likes tricking campers into saying forbidden words.

Counselor Lenel (koun´səl lər len´l): Campfire Stories and Campfire Songs Counselor. From *House Cheer*.

Counselor Markus (koun´səl lər mär´kus): Cabin counselor for *House Joy*.

Counselor Melinda (koun´səl lər mə lin´du): Music counselor. Kind, but somewhat naïve. She's cabin counselor to *House Jolly*.

Counselor / Psychiatrist / Nurse Pamela / Pam Hilton (koun´səl lər / sī kī´ə trist / nurs pam el´ə / pam hil´tun): The nurse at the nurse's office. Her nametag says Pam, but she introduces herself as Pamela. It's very confusing.

Craig (crag): An assistant who's only task is to take care of Kevin, a camper with special needs.

Cretin Malefic (krēt´n mə lef´ik): Teacher's supposedly real name. It was likely judged inappropriate for the camp.

Daniel (dan´vəl): The main character. He leads the boys against the camp rules. Originally part of Counselor Melinda's Home Group, he is later forced into Counselor Dave's Home Group and then later into Counselor Delilah's. He is bunked in *House Joy*.

Greg (grə g): One of the two kids to have joined Daniel on his way to the Art Barn. He is part of Counselor Delilah's Home Group. He is bunked in *House Joy*.

Head Counselor Petrel (hed koun´səl lər pet´rel): The leader of the camp. He is cold and calculating. He knows the rules.

Ike (īk): Wendy's partner during Counselor Melinda's music lesson. He's in Counselor Kimberly's Home Group.

Imposter Kimberly (im pәs´tәr kim bur´lē): Someone who is filling in or replacing the original counselor. From *House Glee*.

Jackal (jak´әl): Older kid who went with Mitchel, the kid who called younger kids babies. He is bunked in *House Joy*.

Jiminy (Jim·min´ē): Million Questions Kid. He is bunked in *House Joy*.

Katina (kut´ēnә): Wants to go by Tina. She is part of Counselor Delilah's Home Group.

Kayla (kā´lu): Meliah's friend who left the group at the kickball field. She's in Counselor Kimberly's Home Group.

Kevin (ke´vin): A camper with special needs. He is sent home after breaking the iguana cage in the Nature Center in an attempt to free his lizard friend.

Macey (mās´ē): Part of Counselor Dave's Home Group.

Maran (mär´in): Daniel's mother.

Meliah (me´lī´u): A shy girl who partners with Daniel during Counselor Melinda's music lesson. She knows Daniel from school, but he doesn't remember her. She's in Counselor Kimberly's Home Group.

Michelle (mish´el): The weeping girl. Part of Counselor Dave's Home Group.

Mitchel (mich´ul): He picked on the younger kids in his cabin and called them babies. He is bunked in *House Joy*.

Mr. McGregor (mis´tәr muk´grә gôr): Former owner of the camp.

Mrs. Parker (mis´әs pär´kur): A camp counselor. One in charge of a girl's cabin.

Nate (nāt): A solitary kid forced to watch the Positivity Camp Video.

Naython (nā´thun): Jiminy's older brother and the canoe kid. He is bunked in *House Joy*.

<u>Nobody (nō'bädē):</u> A *cool kid* like Tyler. He tries to ingratiate himself with Wendy and Kayla at the Nature Center. His true name is unknown. Part of Counselor Delilah's Home Group.

<u>Officer Hays (ôf'i sər hāz):</u> An officer that is told to alert Wendy and Daniel's parents of their safety.

<u>Rett (rət):</u> He is one of the younger campers in *House Joy*.

<u>Teacher (tē'chər):</u> The mysterious art teacher only known as Teacher. He does the sign making for the camp's forbidden words.

<u>Terry (ter'ē):</u> A kid who inspires the *Nein* song as he tells Daniel about his German heritage. He is part of Counselor Delilah's Home Group.

<u>Tina (tēnə):</u> See Katina.

<u>Tyler (tī'lur):</u> The camp's cool kid. He explored the camp with Kayla. He is bunked in *House Joy*. He appears to be in Counselor Kimberly's Home Group, but Daniel has his suspicions.

<u>Wendy (wen'dē):</u> Daniel's camp friend. She leads the girls against the camp rules. Part of Counselor Melinda's Home Group. She's in Counselor Kimberly's Home Group.

<u>Zach (zak):</u> One of the younger campers in *House Joy*.

About the Author

Sarah Maree isn't the nerdiest nerd you've ever met, but she still likes to think of herself as a lover of science, video games, and of course, books. For much of her life, Sarah wanted to be a Marine Biologist. In her senior year of high school, she took a dual credit course in Marine Biology. The class took a trip to Costa Rica to aid in the protection and preservation of the endangered leatherback sea turtles. The experience only strengthened her desire to pursue Marine Biology as a career.

That same year, she enrolled at Indiana Purdue University Fort Wayne (IPFW) with the intent of graduating with a degree in Marine Biology. When the chemistry courses killed that dream, she did some tough soul searching and realized her passion for writing. During her pursuit of an English degree, Sarah took a bookbinding class and quickly fell in love with the art of crafting books. It paired well with her love of writing, and in 2014, she created an Etsy shop to sell her handmade books.

She graduated in 2013 with a bachelor's degree in English, and later that year, she married her first and only love, Nicholas Klein. Combining her love of writing with his video and photography skills, they went into business together. When a severe case of writer's block struck, Sarah began contacting different writers she knew and formed a writing group in 2015. What started out as three members eventually became a larger group of writing friends. Nowadays, Sarah works from home as a social media manager. In her free time, she continues writing and publishing her work on her blog Caffeine is my Muse and crafting books with paper, fabric, and leather.

The original raves from Positivity Camp as seen on the author's blog *Caffeine is my Muse*.

"What?! I need more!!!!"
– Erin Dafforn

"This camp is crazy! I'd go nuts here! . . . Never underestimate the power of the girl's network!"
– Mary Redding

"I love it. Great post! But it's too short!!! I want more!"
– Alicia Rae

"The 42 song was pathetically great. Those poor kids."
– Larkynn de la Fuerza

"What a twist! . . . These counselors are seriously messed up."
– Neri

"Sometimes where you leave us hanging is painful. Lol but love this series…"
– Danielle Larison

"Awesome!"
– Angie Keck